DOMME

CLUB NOIR #0

Onné Andrews

This is a work of fiction. All characters, organizations and events in this novel are products of the author's imagination and are not to be construed as real. Any resemblance to persons, living or dead, is entirely coincidental.

DOMME
(Club Noir #0)

ISBN-13 - 978-1-64918-003-2

Published by Angry Sheep Publishing
Findlay, Ohio

Cover Design by Just Write. Creations and Services
Interior Design by JW Manus

More books by Onné Andrews
(Each series is in suggested reading order)

Secrets

Tied By Lust
Bound By Desire
Taken By Passion
Enslaved By Love
Secrets: The Boxed Set

Club Noir

Domme

Club Noir Marde Gras

Voil Jeanette (Coming soon!)
Bon Temps (Coming soon!)
Noblisse Oblige (Coming soon!)

Naughty Neighbors

Three's Company
Four of a Kind
The Cherry on Top (Coming Soon)

Dirty Dozen

Eat Me
To Punish and Service
Take Me
Dreams of Anubis
Do Unto Others

Educating Lisa

The Professor's Wife
The New Master
The Final Lesson

Horny Holidays

Santa's Gift
Cupid's Arrow
Son of a Bunny (Coming Soon)

Sex and the Single Monster

Everlasting Hope
Zombie's Night Out
Puppy Love (Coming Soon)

For news, sales, and giveaways, join Onné's mailing list or visit Onné's website at www.onneandrews.com You can also check her out on Twitter or Facebook.

(Your information will not be sold, leased or otherwise given to a third party.)

Author's Note: This story takes place thirty years prior to the events in *Tied By Lust*.

Chapter One

For once, the sun shone in London, turning the early May afternoon bright and glorious, while Rick Paine zipped through the city in his convertible. The car was the one luxury he allowed himself. The weather was far too nice to listen to Thatcher drone on about the current recession. Rick twisted the radio knob to off. He understood the prime minister was attempting to rally support in Parliament, but Rick wasn't sure the working class, his own class, would listen to more bullshit. And everyone ignored the growing issues with Iraq.

The delicious smells of the outdoor cafés mixed with petrol fumes. The growl and vibration of his auto's engine didn't overcome the wolf whistles of men trying to gain the attention of the girls in their pastel dresses or the women in their jewel-toned power suits. As much as Rick would have preferred to spend the day whizzing about the countryside in his baby with a beautiful lady at his side, Jamie wouldn't have called him unless the matter was one of life or death.

Rick pulled into the drive for the Royal Britannia Hotel. Like everything else on the West End, its marble, gold trim, and glass was polished to perfection. He climbed out of his car and handed the strange gold coin Jamie had sent him to the valet.

The young man merely nodded as he pocketed the coin and climbed into the driver's seat. Surprisingly, the valet didn't even grind the gears as he accelerated back onto the street and disappeared around the corner.

Rick adjusted his tie and headed into the hotel's main entrance. It was far too warm on a day like this to be wearing his dark grey three-piece suit, but Jamie had insisted on proper business wear for this meeting. Once Rick cleared the revolving door, he immediately attracted the attention of both the hotel's security as well the private guards employed by the hotel's guests scattered around the lobby. This was a damn odd place to meet Jamie, but then, everything Jamie did could be considered odd since he entered politics. Rick kept his hands at his sides. He wouldn't be a bit surprised if the men in the lobby carried illegal firearms as well as legal ones.

At the very least, it was cooler in here with the damn wool suit he wore.

He approached the concierge desk. The girl behind the real wood counter was attractive in a simpering, bottle-blond sort of way. She wore the hotel's uniform, but the scarlet vest had been altered to an ultra-form-fitting level, and her white dress shirt was unbuttoned far enough to display a copious amount of flesh. Definitely not his type.

"May I help you, sir?" She batted her fake eyelashes.

"JWS told me to pick up an envelope here."

The girl's simpering disappeared. "ID, please."

Rick produced his passport. The girl's attention flicked from his photo to him to his photo again before she handed it back to him.

"Thank you, sir." In most of these posh places, she would have addressed him by name, but the Royal Britannia prided itself on its discretion.

His peripheral vision caught the thugs inhabiting the lobby noticeably relax at the concierge's acceptance of him. What the hell was Jamie dragging him into? Oh, God! Had one of Jamie's girlfriends accidentally overdosed during their tryst?

The concierge girl retrieved a plain white envelope from beneath the counter and held it out to Rick. Her simpering smile was back. "Enjoy your visit at the Royal Britannia Hotel, sir."

"Thank you." He slipped her a twenty-pound note as he took the envelope. Both the hotel and private security in the lobby eyed him as one of their own. It didn't mean they were any less suspicious.

Or potentially dangerous.

He crossed to an unoccupied niche that didn't have any windows before he slid his finger beneath the flap. The envelope contained a black key card and a single slip of paper that read, "Come on up. J.H.W-S."

Rick had guarded enough celebrities to know what the black key card meant. If Jamie was shagging some pop tartlet on the side, there would definitely be hell to pay, from Rick himself long before Beth found out about it. He really never understood Jamie's need to cheat on his perfectly lovely wife who accepted him as he was. However, Jamie seemed determined to prove his manhood after losing his leg in the Falklands by screwing any woman who would let him.

Pushing the old arguments aside, Rick strode to the bank of lifts. No one followed him or waited for a car. He stabbed the button, and the doors for the last lift parted as if waiting specifically for him. Nerves on edge, he entered and slid the key card into the slot above the controls. The light blinked green, the doors silently closed, and the lift rose.

When the lift doors parted again, Rick found himself face-to-face with two men who made his one hundred-eighty-five-centimeters and thirteen-stone frame appear scrawny. They stood in front of the two doors leading into the main part of the private suite.

"Identification," the man on his right demanded with a vaguely Saudi accent, and he held out his huge palm.

Once again, Rick reached into his jacket pocket. The security men tensed. Rick slowed his movements as he produced his passport. The man on the right took much longer to examine his credentials than the concierge girl had. He showed it to his partner who nodded.

Without a word, the security guard returned Rick's passport and opened one of the suite doors. Low voices conversed inside. Taking the invitation, Rick entered while he replaced his passport in his pocket.

The suite's sitting room was larger than Rick's entire flat. And a lot cleaner. The decorative flowers on the walls were hand-painted, not wallpaper. The trim was real varnished mahogany. His shoes sank into the rich carpet.

M.P. James "Jamie" Henry Wynton-Smythe's familiar lanky form rose from the couch facing the entryway, a wide grin split his face. "It's about time you got here."

Like Rick, Jamie wore a three-piece suit, but his was navy blue. His receding hairline managed to stick out at odd angles no matter what grooming products he used. And Jamie's smile didn't quite reach his eyes, which meant something was very, very wrong.

But it was the man with Jamie who drew Rick's attention. Faddil El Ahmed, Emir of Kutom. One of the few Middle Eastern leaders who allied his nation with Western Europe and had since the Second World War. He'd been featured quite extensively in the BBC newscasts the last few nights thanks to his talks with the United Kingdom's prime minister over oil and arms.

Despite his years, the emir's spine was straight without being rigid, his body fit beneath the expensive, pale grey tailored suit he wore. If it weren't for the crow's feet and white streaks in his hair and beard, he would have looked closer to Rick's own age.

"Your Majesty, Minister." Rick shook hands with both men. Jamie's constant lessons concerning protocol and etiquette came in handy at times.

"Please, sit, Mister Paine." The emir indicated the couch opposite where Jamie had been sitting. Once the older gentleman resumed his seat on the matching armchair, Rick and Jamie sat.

The emir rang a little gold bell on the side table next to him. A servant brought out a tray containing a steaming pot with bowls of cream and sugar and three cups. Both Jamie and Rick passed on the emir's offer of coffee, though he poured himself a tiny cup. The aroma stated how strong the concoction was.

"May I inquire as to the reason for this meeting, sir?" Rick flicked an uncertain glance at his old friend.

"You are here at my request." The emir leaned against the back of his chair. "I have need of a security expert here in London, Mister Paine."

"Surely your own people or Minister Wynton-Smythe—"

The emir held up his hand. "It is more complicated than my personal security. I have need of someone with a reputation for discretion to protect an associate here in London."

This was not going to end well. Rick rubbed his right eyebrow. "With all due respect, sir, I'm not the person to watch your mistress."

Jamie gave him the watch-your-manners glare, but Rick really didn't care at this point. The emir, however, seemed amused.

He turned to Jamie. "I like him. It will take a strong-willed person to perform this job." He picked up a manila folder that sat next to his coffee tray. "Please look at these before you make up your mind, Mister Paine."

Rick flipped through the pages. The first one appeared to be a copy of a standard love letter addressed to "Beloved J". The next made the writer seem desperate and pathetic. The following three grew progressively more threatening and violent. None of them were signed. All of them mentioned that the writer knew a secret about this "Beloved J".

He looked up at the emir. "Have you contacted Scotland Yard about these?"

"No." The emir shook his head. "Johanna refuses to do so. She's currently a senior house officer at Tower Hospital. She's concerned the scandal would affect her career and possibly my own position."

Rick blinked at that revelation. A doctor? So, she wasn't some bird looking to line her nest with a rich man. He already respected this Johanna.

He handed the folder back to the emir. "Who is she, and what do you expect me to do?"

"Right now, she's very angry, and she doesn't expect you to do a bloody thing," a woman snapped.

Rick twisted on the couch to find a woman stalking into the living area from one of the suite's bedrooms. She was tall with legs that wouldn't quit, even without her impossibly high heels. Hips curved into a small waist accented by a prim skirt. Her blouse couldn't hide her lovely assets on top either. Blue eyes flashed lightning, but all he could think about was how much he wanted to see her chestnut hair flow across her shoulders instead of pinned up.

He belatedly rose when the other two men stood. What was it about her that made all of his manners flee?

She marched to a halt beside the emir's chair and glared at him. "I told you to stay out of this, Faddil. It's not about you. Some idiot has his knickers in a twist over having yet another woman in the medical field."

"No, Doctor," Rick said evenly. "It's about you, and from what I just read, if you don't take this seriously, it will escalate until someone gets hurt. His Majesty doesn't want you to be that person."

"And who might you be?" she said archly.

"This is Mister Richard Paine," the emir replied. "Rick, may I introduce Doctor Johanna Ridgeley?"

A sly smile crossed her face, one that sent an electric thrill through Rick's entire body. "Paine. How appropriate."

Chapter Two

Johanna recognized the look of desire on Richard Paine's face the moment she walked into Faddil's sitting room. The need to submit warred against society's demands on men, and he probably didn't even know why he had that reaction to her. It was a shame he would merely be a thorn in her side.

She turned back to Faddil. "Why are you interfering in my life?"

"Because one of us needs to take your safety seriously," he answered calmly.

They'd kept their relationship on a professional level for years until he met the lovely Gamila. Training her had been an enjoyable experience for all three of them.

Johanna eyed Paine again. "Personal security expert?"

He nodded.

She faced Faddil again. "I can't afford his services, Faddil. Nor am I accepting any money from you to pay his fee."

"Then consider him a gift, my treasure." He lifted her hand and kissed the back of it.

Such intimacy in front of strangers bothered her. She had very strict rules concerning their relationship over the years. Why was Faddil breaking their agreement now? Or was that the real problem? Was he using her harasser as an excuse to resume their intimate relationship?

Johanna breathed deeply to clear her mind. "You cannot simply present a man to me as a gift, Faddil. This is the United Kingdom, not Kutom."

Paine took one step toward her. "Doctor Ridgeley, allow me to have twenty-four hours with you."

She raised an eyebrow at his presumption.

Despite his self-assured voice, the tips of his ears pinked as he realized he'd overstepped with her. "To evaluate your precautions and habits in order to reassure the emir of your safety."

She glared at him. "You're not the first person to impinge on His Majesty's largesse."

"And he wouldn't have asked Minister Wynton-Smythe for a personal recommendation if he didn't believe you might be at some risk," Paine replied. "I'll do a twenty-four hour evaluation free of charge. I'll then present my findings and any suggestions to you and His Majesty." He gestured towards the folder containing copies of the letters sent to her. "If you're right, the correspondence means nothing. No harm is done, and the matter is settled."

"But of course, you'll find some reason to continue your protection of me," she mocked. It took a great deal of self-control to keep from saying what else she thought. Too many people tried to worm their way into poor Faddil's life to further their own agendas. She would not be used by one of them.

Instead of Paine, it was Minister Wynton-Smythe who became offended. "My good Doctor, Emir Faddil asked me for someone in the U.K. with experience who has the utmost integrity and discretion. Rick is that man. I will not have you make spurious accusations concerning his character."

"Rick?" Her gaze swept over Paine. His suit hinted at regular exercise for the body underneath, but he was lithe, which meant he probably ran or swam. He was tall, but not overly so. The precision conservative cut of his dark hair insinuated a military background. "Why not use 'Dick' for your nickname?"

"It's a little too close to a certain disgraced American president for my taste," he replied smoothly.

"And if I call you 'Richard'?"

"Frankly, I don't give a damn what you call me as long as it doesn't endanger you, Doctor."

Interesting. Most people were very particular about how they're addressed. Yet, he acquiesced to her preference in front of higher ranking males in the room, something a modern male rarely did without fear of losing his appearance of strength. It made Richard even more of an enigma.

But as attractive of a prospect he appeared to be, she had the career she wanted since she was a little girl. She simply didn't have time to explore any other new challenges, no matter how much they appealed to her personally. A pity she hadn't met Richard at another time in their lives.

However, his deference had earned a bit of kindness. "Richard, I appreciate you volunteering your time and services on my behalf," she said gently. "However, I spend a great deal of my time at the hospital these days. The person sending these letters isn't going to try anything in such a public place."

"With all due respect, Doctor." A fierceness filled his dark eyes. "The letter writer could be one of your medical associates."

"Please, my mistress." Faddil reached for her hand, but she arched an eyebrow at the attempt to touch her without permission twice in a row. He reconsidered the idea and let his hand fall to his side. "Allow Mister Paine to ensure your flat is secure, if for no other reason, to settle my own fears for your safety."

It was so rare for her former sub to beg outside of their private times. For him to do so in front of witnesses, any one of whom could use this truth against Faddil, indicated how unsettled he was in this matter. And when a sub was this unsettled, he often did foolish things.

"All right," she said finally and held out her palm. He took it in both of his hands and kissed it.

However, her attention remained on Richard Paine. Disappointment flashed across his face before he resumed his professional air. In turn, a little disappointment twinged within her that he'd made assumptions about her without bothering to discover the truth. Maybe he was like the majority of untrainable men after all.

Ten minutes later, Johanna sat in the passenger seat of Paine's classic convertible. He'd been courteous and gentlemanly to her when he ushered her to the lobby and into his automobile, acting like a proper escort by opening and closing doors. Nor did he attempt to touch her without permission. However, he had remained silent in their drive through the streets of London.

"May I ask you a question?" he said finally as they waited at a traffic light.

"That depends," she murmured.

"Then let me preface my question." His attention flicked between the mirrors and the windscreen. "I'm puzzling out whether you're the real target of your correspondent or if the emir is. Are you his mistress?"

"Isn't that what he called me in front of you?"

"Yes, but I'd prefer to hear it from you."

Amusement trickled through her. "Then that depends on your meaning of the word."

"Do you have a sexual relationship with him?"

"Why does that matter?"

His fingers tapped the steering wheel. "If the emir cares for you, then perhaps he is the target."

"'Cares for' as in, does he love me?"

"Yes."

She chuckled. "You have mentioned two separate elements. People can have sex with those they don't care about, and they can care about those they don't have sex with."

"Are you deliberately trying to muddy the issue?" He glanced at her.

"No, I'm simply trying to ascertain what you truly wish to know."

"Why do women have to play coy over a simple question?" he grumbled.

"Because men often judge us for having the same desires they do, and they do not wish to compete with us."

He blew out an exasperated breath. "Can we please start over if I promise not to judge you for sleeping with the emir?"

Disappointment hit Johanna like a blow. Teasing Richard Paine could be a full-time sport. Why couldn't he have come along at a different point in her life?

"I have never slept with the emir."

"As in sleeping in the same bed or as his cock has never entered your vagina?"

She couldn't help laughing again. "Aren't you a quick one, Richard? The truthful answer to both questions is no."

He frowned as if he wasn't quite sure he believed her. "But you've had sex?"

"Now, you're asking whether I'm a virgin." Despite her irritation with Faddil, she found she enjoyed verbally jousting with Richard Paine.

"No, I'm trying to figure out your relationship with the emir," he said.

"Because you're trying to ascertain who the target is." She considered her options. If this was about embarrassing or harming Faddil, she would be remiss in dismissing Richard's efforts. "Yes, we did have a personal relationship."

"So you were having sex with him?"

"There's a great many ways a person can find pleasure without intercourse."

His attention flicked toward her then back to the street. However, he didn't have the dismissive attitude or the expression of distaste as he worked out the truth.

"So you are his dominatrix," Richard breathed.

"I was." She watched his face carefully. He was handling the news far better than she expected. No signs of disgust or loathing. "Does that bother you?"

He cleared his throat while he kept his eyes on the street. "No, ma'am. As I said, I'm trying to understand who the real target of the harassing letters is. Given cultural norms and differences, your preferences might explain the threat to expose your secrets."

Johanna chuckled. "Given cultural norms as you put it, why don't you think my correspondent isn't trying to embarrass Faddil?"

Richard frowned. "I haven't completely ruled out the possibility. Does anyone know the specificities of your relationship?"

"Only his primary bodyguards are aware of Faddil's. . .needs." She considered the situation. The last thing she wanted was harm to come to Faddil in any shape or form. "One of them may have a private objection to Faddil's activities."

"Did you two always meet at the same hotel?" He signaled a right turn.

"No." It was her turn to frown. "Prior to the death of his father, we met at a private club that caters to our particular play. After he became emir, his chief of security insisted we meet at his hotel for Faddil's safety."

"That's understandable," Richard murmured. "Even a private club would be difficult to investigate thoroughly without revealing the reason why. Even then, that type of a club would rigorously defend their clients' privacy. How is your relationship with his chief of security?"

Johanna contemplated his question. "Faddil's safety is Hosni's foremost concern." She smiled at the memory. "When Faddil's father had his stroke, Hosni and I had a long conversation about the future of the then-crown prince and Kutom."

"Let me guess," Richard said. "Hosni was worried about a possible scandal with political or religious turmoil undermining the emir's authority during the transition."

"And the subsequent implications of Kutom's foreign relations," she added.

"Is that when you stopped seeing the emir?"

She sighed. Playing with Faddil had been fun and educational for them both. While she still held affection for him, she'd known all along their relationship couldn't be permanent.

"We still have lunch together when he's in London and his schedule allows," she murmured. "As for the other activities, yes, we stopped after I trained my substitute. His third wife has an aptitude for the type of experience he needs. I spent three months teaching her."

"How'd the first two wives handle the third wife taking more of his attention?"

"Not more attention," Johanna corrected. "A different type. The other two believe Faddil and I had a conventional affair. Gamila loves him too much to reveal his secret to the others. And their activities give her a sense of satisfaction she would not have otherwise as the lowest ranking wife."

Richard remained silent until he parked in front of her flat. She loved the Georgian white brick building the moment she saw it. The austere, clean lines had a certain discipline while the inside was gloriously rich with detail.

Much like herself.

He shut off the engine and held out his hand. "May I please have your keys?"

She turned to him and narrowed her eyes. "Why?"

"I want to check out the building and your flat specifically." It was a statement, not a command, but the words still grated along her ego.

"That is where I draw the line, Mister Paine." She pulled the latch to open the car door. "I'll tolerate your presence in my life for the next twenty-four hours at Faddil's request, but I will not let you take control of it."

Johanna slung her purse over her left forearm, climbed out of his vehicle, and headed for the main door. Why was she letting him rile her? No, she couldn't deal with the temptation he presented. She was now a physician. She'd put away that part of herself in order to help people who couldn't help themselves.

Richard caught up with her and grabbed her elbow. After a sharp look from her, he released his hold.

"I'm only trying to ensure your safety, Miss Ridgely."

"It's *Doctor* Ridgely, and you don't need a copy of my keys for that." She unlocked the main door and marched up the staircase.

"I didn't ask for a copy," he snapped as he jogged up the steps behind her. "I asked to borrow your keys temporarily—"

"In order to make a copy." She glared at him while she slid the key into the door for her flat, twisted the key, and shoved open the door.

"No, I wanted you safely in my vehicle—" He scowled at something behind her.

She turned and caught sight of what had interrupted him. Her heart threatened to climb out of her throat.

An inflatable doll sat on one of her kitchen chairs in the middle of the living room floor. It was clothed in her favorite leather dress. A brunette wig sat on the doll's head, the cut mirroring her own hair. The figure was also gagged and duct-taped to the chair. The worst part was the words scrawled across the skirt of the dress in her scarlet nail polish.

I CAN'T WAIT TO SEE YOU LIKE THIS

Chapter Three

Rick half-expected Johanna to scream, but after the initial shock crossed her face, rage replaced it.

"How dare they!" She marched toward the doll.

"Don't." He grabbed her elbow and pulled her back to the door-frame. "We are going downstairs. Would one of your neighbors let us use their phone?"

He thought she would fight him, like she had with everything else in the brief hour and a half since they'd met, but she took a deep breath and nodded. The rage was still evident, but she seemed to have it under control. "Mrs. Cresswell will be home. She's our landlady."

He guided Johanna away from the apartment. For the first time, she didn't argue with him.

A quick conversation first with Hosni, and then with the emir, emphasized they didn't want the police involved. Neither did Johanna, once she had a cup of tea and gotten over the initial shock and fury.

"Are you sure that is a good idea, my dear?" Mrs. Cresswell's face wrinkled even more with concern. Her hair matched the color of the white Persian that lay curled in her blue-skirted lap. Rick would have sworn the cat glared at him personally. "If someone broke into the building and your flat—"

"They didn't break in," Rick said before he sipped his own tea. After the conversations with the men from Kutom, he'd examined all doors and windows. "Does anyone else besides the two of you and the other tenants have keys?"

"Only my nephew Isaac Beckwith," Mrs. Cresswell stated firmly. "He handles the minor maintenance. If there's a matter he cannot handle, I let in the outside repairman and I keep watch over him while he's working. I also have the locks changed on each flat when a tenant moves out."

"You take your tenants' security very seriously, Mrs. Cresswell," Rick commented.

"Because everyone deserves a peaceful home, Mister Paine." The fierce look in her eyes reminded him of Johanna. So fierce, he wondered what event had bonded the two women.

"What is the name and number of your locksmith?" Rick pulled a notebook from his coat pocket.

"Surely, you don't think he or his staff has anything to do with this?" Mrs. Cresswell frowned and cocked her head.

"I need to check out all possibilities," Rick said firmly. "Including your nephew Isaac. Whoever is doing this is probably just trying to scare Doctor Ridgeley, but I don't want anything to happen to her, and I'm sure you don't either."

The older woman shook her head. "Of course not." She set her cat on the floor. "Let me get the locksmith's card for you."

Of course the damn thing stalked over and rubbed itself against his legs, leaving a trail of white fur along his dark grey slacks.

Chapter Four

An hour later, Johanna's belief that she had calmed and collected herself shattered as Richard made more of a mess of her living area. She tried to keep her irritability from leaking into her voice, but it trailed like blood through water. "What do you hope to accomplish, or have you simply watched too many telly programmes?"

Richard looked up from where he sat in the middle of her living room. After he'd donned white cotton gloves, he used what looked like a powder foundation brush to spread a silvery white dust over the doll and her formerly favorite leather dress. Even though he'd borrowed an old sheet from her, the bloody dust was getting everywhere.

"If I can retrieve a clean fingerprint, a friend at Scotland Yard can check it for me." He continued to spread the blasted powder and peer occasionally at the doll's plastic skin.

"And how long would that take?" She suspected she knew, but she wanted to see if he'd tell her the truth.

He frowned. "Unfortunately, it could take a couple of months, and that's assuming your visitor has been booked before."

"Two months?"

"Unfortunately." He looked at her expectantly.

"What?"

His right eyebrow rose, but he didn't seem to be mocking her. "I'm waiting for your tirade about how I can't interfere with your life for that length of time."

"Is that your intent here?" She watched him carefully. Did he expect to use this incident as an excuse to stay in her flat? "To continue interfering with my life?"

He paused and rested his arm holding the powder brush on his knee. "I think you need to take this matter seriously. It has gone beyond mere anonymous protestations of affection."

Johanna wasn't quite sure what to do. No doubt Faddil had vetted this man thoroughly. The last thing she wanted was to show any weakness to a submissive. Or did Richard even know what he was?

But he seemed rather sincere about her safety. The doll proved whoever sent her those letters was willing to commit criminal acts to further his obsession. While she believed she could take care of herself, she wasn't fool enough to think for one minute she was safe from someone who obviously viewed her as prey.

"I'll get the original letters for you." She rose and stalked over to her desk, conscious of the way he watched her. Her fingers trembled as she yanked open the bottom drawer and tugged the clear plastic zippered bag from the back. She squelched her nerves, or tried to as she crossed to Richard.

He accepted the bag and looked up at her. "Did you touch them with your bare hands?"

"The first two." She sat on the edge of her fold-out couch. "I was caught unawares by the first one. The second was on the top of the stack when I withdrew the day's post from my box."

"The others?" His right eyebrow rose to emphasize his question.

"I used my kitchen tongs," she admitted. "I guess I watch the same crime dramas."

"When did you have time for anything fun while you were in medical school?" He smiled and unzipped the bag.

"Not so much during classes," Johanna said. "But now I splurge when Prime Suspect airs."

He glanced up from examining the postal marks. "So you like crime dramas?"

"More like looking for tips for dealing with a male-dominated profession whose members want nothing more than to see me fail." Johanna bit her tongue to keep her expression passive. She never would reveal so much of her bitterness, or herself, in such a simple conversation with a sub.

"Is that what you think I want?" He appeared genuinely confused.

She shrugged as nonchalantly as she could. "I have no idea what you want other than the hefty sum I'm sure Faddil promised you."

"I'd charge the Queen herself the same rate if she requested my services as I would for one of your nurses," he said brusquely.

"And what about the beggar on the street? What would you charge him?"

"A homeless person is already at the bottom of the social pile, Doctor Ridgeley." He stared at the doll for a moment before his attention returned to her. "This is someone who is trying to exert power over you without your consent. If that happened during a private session, what would you do?"

Johanna resisted the urge to shiver. "I would defend myself."

"Who was it, and what happened?" Richard asked quietly.

"I can't tell you. The club I belong to requires the utmost discretion." She lifted her chin. What was it about this man? Why did he evade her defenses so easily?

"That's exactly why the emir hired me. Anything you tell me will be held in the strictest confidence, Doctor, but as I said to Mrs. Cresswell, I need to follow every possible lead."

Even though Richard made perfect sense, Johanna hesitated. Old habits died hard. Especially since she worked so hard to keep her personal and professional lives separate.

"Johanna, this may be a case of revenge for a scene that went wrong." He waved his brush to indicate the doll and ruined dress. "I wouldn't intrude on your privacy otherwise."

"There was a man at Club Noir." She clasped her hands together. "The private club both Faddil and I belong to."

He nodded for her to continue.

"Some younger son of a peer. He—" Her mouth went dry at the memory, and she stared at the doll. "It was the only time I ever lost control of a sub. Ethan claimed he wanted to play, but he insisted I address him as the Honourable Slave. Things escalated to the point he became physical. I hit the security button. But before they arrived . . ."

"Did he hurt you?"

Johanna met Richard's gaze. "He pulled out a few strands of hair when he tried to force me to suck his cock. I bit him."

Richard managed to wince and chuckle at the same time. "Serves the wanker right. Did the emir get him sacked from the club?"

"Actually, that was the event that precipitated Faddil asking to serve me." She smiled. "However, the board did rescind Ethan's membership. And Faddil is not and has never been on the board of directors at the club."

"It doesn't mean he can't exert some influence." Rick paused before he said, "I have to ask—"

"Ethan Armstrong-Home." It was surprising how much lighter she felt by revealing that bit of unpleasantness.

"Is that the real reason you don't want me in your home?" He tilted his head as he regarded her. "You're concerned I might be equally ill-mannered?"

"The thought crossed my mind," she admitted. "I don't allow my personal and professional lives to intermix."

"Except for the emir." It was a statement, not a question.

"He has been the exception," she confessed. "And I admit I am fonder of him than I should be. In a way, I'm thankful." She gestured at the doll. "This message appears to be solely aimed at me. I don't want to see Faddil harmed."

"What about Mrs. Cresswell or the other tenants?" Richard asked.

Johanna frowned. "Our culprit only broke into my place."

"But he had a key to the building." Richard frowned back at her. "He could have gotten into one of the other flats." He held up one of the envelopes. "This isn't someone who's exactly rational."

"To him, what he's doing is perfectly rational."

"Or her," he replied. "Did you have any problems with any of the women at the club?"

Johanna couldn't help smiling. For all of Richard's military bearing, he could think beyond the binary. "No, I don't believe so. If one of the female members has an issue with me, I am not aware of it."

"When was the last time you frequented the club?" Again, he was curious. She still detected no hint of unease or jealousy in regards to what she was or her tastes.

"My last year in medical school." She stared at the porthos hanging above the tiny table in the alcove next to the kitchen. The dangling brown leaves needed to be trimmed. Maybe the odd letters had thrown her off more than she cared to admit if she had been that lax in caring for the plant. She turned back to Richard. "A little over two years ago."

"Someone's resentment could fester that long before action is taken." His brow crinkled. "However, this may be someone you encounter in your every day routine."

"Like Mrs. Cresswell?" She smiled.

He grinned in return. "As I said, I won't rule anyone out yet." His expression sobered. "Does she know about your personal life?"

Johanna hesitated for a moment. He already knew about Faddil and the club. No sense in acting coy now. "Yes."

"What about the other tenants?" he asked.

"I've never told them, if that's what you're asking," she said.

"Do you speak with any of them? More than a casual greeting in the hallway?"

"There's Felicity in the other upstairs unit. She's a solicitor. Both of us work quite a bit, so I rarely see her." Johanna tapped her finger against her lips. "Stella used to live in the downstairs unit across from Mrs. Cresswell, but she moved out last fall when she got married. She was a kindergarten teacher. I haven't met the girl who just moved in. I believe Mrs. Cresswell said her name is Monica."

Richard nodded. "That gives me a starting place." He shook his head. "I've only got one partial print off your dress."

"It's more than what Hosni was able to retrieve from—" She turned and glared at the ringing phone. This was her one day off. If this were the hospital, she would ram a probe up someone's backside. She grabbed the receiver from the end table and stabbed the appropriate button.

"Hello?"

"Did you receive my present, my beloved J?" The raspy voice sent a chill through her.

She turned to Richard and mouthed, "It's him."

He pantomimed another receiver. She pointed to her bedroom. Normally, she wouldn't let a potential sub into such an intimate space.

But Richard wasn't a potential sub. He was here to investigate whoever had broken into her flat.

"Don't tell me you have a ball gag in your pretty little mouth?" the raspy voice said. Whoever it was, they didn't notice the subtle click when Richard picked up the receiver at her bedside table. Or they chose not to acknowledge it.

"I don't appreciate my belongings being ruined," she said calmly.

"Don't you like being the plaything for once?" the voice cooed. "I'm enjoying this game."

"A real game is one that's mutually agreed on." Johanna dug the nails of her right hand into the flesh of her palm. She couldn't let this bastard know they were getting under her skin. "You did not ask nicely."

"You don't ask nicely either," the raspy voice snarled. "That's the problem with you bitches. It's all take. Take. Take. Someday soon though, you're going to find out what it's like when someone takes from you."

The disconnected line buzzed in her ear.

Chapter Five

Rick replaced the trimline's receiver back into its cradle. A Dominant like Johanna would never have let him in her bedroom under normal circumstances. But then, these were most definitely not normal circumstances by any means.

Like the rest of her apartment, everything in her bedroom was practical and functional. Nothing frilly or pink or flowered. In fact, it reminded him of his own flat. She didn't adhere to society's standards for women.

Which was why Johanna's harasser was obsessed with putting her in her place.

Rick stalked out to Johanna's living room. "You shouldn't have taunted him."

"I didn't simply taunt him." Her icy blue gaze could have shattered steel. "I was trying to keep him on the line. Give you a chance to learn something about him, or maybe even one of us hearing something in the background that would give us a clue as to who he is."

Her words took him aback. He knew she was a smart one, but her psychological insight made him pause.

"My apologies, Doctor." He inclined his head. "Most of my clients react out of fear in a situation such as this. Scared people make mistakes."

A wry smile tilted her the perfect bow of her lips. "Apology accepted, but you are right. I'd be a fool not to be concerned about this person.

On the other hand, I hoped by antagonizing him a bit, he would make a mistake."

"What makes you think it was a him?"

She inhaled and exhaled, the rise and fall of her chest making him think things about her that he shouldn't. She was a client for chrissakes!

"The language he used," she said finally. "Women don't use the word "bitch" the way men do. And he lumped me in with other women he has encountered, whom he felt had taken from him."

Rick nodded. "That's what I got from him, too. Let's make a list of men you know. Someone who's had an ugly divorce or bad breakup."

She held up her right index finger. "First, I will make us some tea while you clean up the mess you made in my living room. Then we'll work on your list."

The peach tea relaxed Rick as he sat at Johanna's small kitchen table. It was covered with a pristine white tablecloth and two woven blue place mats. The salt and pepper shakers were precisely aligned with the napkin holder. Johanna was a well-ordered woman. Practically on the verge of being obsessive.

Which was the only reason she agreed to his presence. She tasked him with getting rid of the disorder, i.e. her shadow.

Part of him wondered what had happened early in her life that caused her to need such a level of control. While he would normally ask, Johanna was the type who would view such a question as a threat to her control. She'd refuse any additional assistance, and more than likely she would end up a victim of her stalker.

Which raised an interesting question. Why was the stalker focused on her? Mistress Johanna may be prey Scotland Yard wouldn't care about. However, if anything happened to Doctor Ridgeley, that would garner a great deal more press. Unless the stalker had a plan where she would never be found. The thought chilled him to his core.

Rick started two lists, both of which his client was likely to argue about with him.

"I'd like to put recording devices on your phones," he said.

"Must you?"

"We'll need evidence to present to the Yard for your stalker to be prosecuted for threatening you." When she still looked uncertain, he laid down his pen. "If there are other clients like the emir, whom you are seeing or have seen in the past, and they might call here, I need to know."

"Why?" she asked before she took a sip of her tea.

"If they are innocent, I'll protect your privacy, both yours and theirs." He searched her face, looking for a sign she was taking him seriously. "However, it's entirely possible a client could be your harasser. Someone who's jealousy of your other clients has become an obsession."

She exhaled without blowing out her cheeks like most people would and leaned back in her chair. "No, I'm not currently seeing anyone, in a professional or a personal capacity. Like I said before, I don't have the time with my medical training. This is the first real day off I've had in a while."

"Surely, NHS doesn't work you to the bone like an American hospital would?"

She smiled. "Most of my days off are spent on mundane household tasks. Both mine and Mrs. Cresswell's." Interesting. Johanna wasn't as tough as she liked to project. Or did she only have issues with showing her softer side with men?

"What about a past client besides Mister Armstrong-Home?" He tapped his pen against his pad.

"Or a past trainer?" She smiled and pointedly watched him tap the pen.

With an effort, he forced himself to stop. She seemed to see right through to his soul. And for some reason, the idea of her with another man bothered him.

"Unfortunately, yes," Rick murmured.

From her little frown, she was obviously taking his question seriously. "There was a trainer who believed no woman was truly a dominant, but that's been nearly ten years ago."

"Before you met the emir?" He scribbled the information on his notepad.

"Yes." Her frown deepened, and she set down her cup on its saucer with a harsh *clink*. "Why do your questions keep coming back to Faddil?"

"Because it's entirely possible your harasser feared crossing the emir until now."

"Or you still believe I'm merely a pawn against him." She sighed.

"Given the phone call earlier, I'm beginning to doubt that theory." He deliberately tapped his pen against his pad again.

This time, she ignored his actions and stared out the window at the tiny garden behind the massive house. From her pursed lips, she definitely disliked talking about herself, much less her past. She had the tense bearing of a feral cat who knew she was overmatched and was about to race away from danger.

"Who was the trainer who went too far, Doctor Ridgeley?" he said softly.

"Ian Addington," Johanna murmured. She continued to stare out the window. "He recommended my membership to Club Noir. I agreed to his conditions."

"What conditions?"

"I had to act as his sub in order to learn to be a good mistress," she said bitterly.

"That's utter bullshit."

"I know that now." She turned to face him again.

"However . . ." Rick prompted.

A rueful smile crossed her face. "Ian thought no one was around.

One of the safety masters saw him hitting me with his fists and pulled him off me. I have to admit the black eye and split lip were the most effective lessons I ever learned."

Part of Rick wanted to hunt down the bloody bastard and beat the pulp out of him. One did not dominate through fear and violence. He would have never submitted to such a cruel mistress. Why did other men expect women to do so?

"I take it he was expelled from Club Noir as well?"

Johanna nodded. "I didn't lodge the complaint. Since the safety master witnessed his actions, Ian was automatically expelled that very night. He blamed me for not supporting him."

"What the bloody hell did he expect?" Rick blurted.

"An apt expression." Johanna's lips quirked in a slight smile. "When the directors and the safety masters asked me, I said I had not agreed to blood play."

Rick couldn't help it. He roared at her description. When his humor died, he looked at her.

"The fool didn't realize what he could have had. Any man worth his salt would consider himself lucky to serve a Domme like you."

Chapter Six

The air froze in Johanna's lungs. So, Richard knew exactly what he was. However, she was in no place in her life to take on a new sub.

For now, anyway. Not with another year as an SHO and her post-graduate exams to be admitted to the Membership of the Royal Colleges of Physicians. Yet, she found Richard fascinating in the few hours she'd known him. Minister Wynton-Smythe mentioned he had served with Richard in the British Army. He'd definitely would be an interesting challenge. He wanted to please, but on his own terms. Training him—

Wasn't something she should even be considering. Not now. Not between her harasser and her medical career. But when was the last time she had a little fun? If only she'd met Richard at another time in her life. And now was definitely not the situation to pursue anything.

Not when someone was threatening her. She couldn't, no, she would never put her sub in danger. Richard's role as her security agent meant she would have to let him do his job, which may mean placing himself between her and her harasser.

Johanna cleared her throat. "Anyway, those are the only ones who I've knowingly had issues with."

"What about your supervisor at the hospital?" Rick said. "You mentioned dealing with colleagues who dislike working with women."

"Doctor Bennett is demanding with all of the SHOs he supervises." She frowned. "Other than he asked me out after his wife left him.

I pointed out both of our careers were at risk if I accepted, and I didn't wish to deprive future physicians of his knowledge and skills. He seemed to accept my refusal graciously."

"On the surface," Richard said.

Johanna sighed. "He's done nothing openly or otherwise to retaliate against me if that is what you are trying to infer."

"All right," he conceded. "What about your fellow house officers?"

She waved her hand. "The same sort of insults and snubs I received in medical school. They managed to drive out another female intern in our first year at Tower."

"That's not right." Richard rubbed his jaw.

"Can you tell me it would be different in the army?" She cocked her head, waiting for him to lie to her.

He shook his head wearily. "No, some of my colleagues have rather old-fashioned views, but I respect the hell out of anyone who can make it through basic training, male or female." He gave her a wary look, and she automatically tensed. She wasn't going to like what he was about to say, and he knew it. "When is your next shift?"

"Tomorrow morning. Seven a.m. Oncology ward."

He nodded. "I'll have Jamie pull some strings."

Anger surged through her. "You are not following me through rounds," she ground out. "That is inappropriate. Not to mention disruptive to the hospital's function."

"I can stay out of your way."

"You must certainly be joking," she said. "What happened to you being discreet and protecting my privacy? You will stand out and draw loads of attention by following me around the hospital."

"We don't have to tell anyone I'm your private security," he said. "We could say I'm a documentary filmmaker."

"Oh, that will go over well with the senior resident," she said sarcastically. The smooth veneer she presented to the world cracked, and for once, she wasn't sure how to regain control.

"Would you prefer I wear a white coat and pretend I'm an observer from a hospital in Germany?" His eyes twinkled. "I'm sure no one would question me," he added with a thick Bavarian accent.

She couldn't stop the chortle that rolled from her throat at his act. Richard Paine had a unique talent for breaking her walls. Yet another reason training him would be a difficult proposition.

He grinned at her lightened mood. "Since this was your day off and I am imposing, let me cook dinner for you while you relax."

"I don't have a whole lot in my cupboards," she replied. Which was true. She simply didn't have the time or energy to prepare anything when she arrived home after a shift at the hospital.

"One thing about being in the army, you learn to get creative with what you have." He rose. "Let me retrieve my bag from the boot, and I'll get started."

With her first bite, Johanna had to admit Richard was true to his word. He somehow turned stale bread, butter, cheese and eggs into a delightfully seasoned soufflé.

"If you ever decide to change careers, you really should become a chef," she said.

He laughed. "No, thank you. Jamie's wife runs a restaurant. I see the hours she puts in, and I rather like my personal time."

"You and Minister Wynton-Smythe are total opposites. How did you two become such great friends?"

"Two months in the Falkland Islands will make even the strangest of comrades friends in the end." Richard's wry smile said far more had happened than he was willing to talk about with her.

"Did you know him before the war?" she asked.

"Only as a major pain in my backside." He forked another bite into his mouth.

"Was he your commanding officer?"

Richard finished chewing and swallowed before he answered. "No. It's simply that classism is alive and well in the U.K. We make fun of India's caste system, but deep down, we're no different."

"Until you have bullets whizzing at you?"

He nodded. "What about you? What made you decide on medical school?"

"I read about Elizabeth Blackwell when I was a child, everything she went through to become a doctor." Johanna shrugged and cut another bite of soufflé. "I wanted to help people like she did."

Richard's gaze cut through her. "Blackwell became a doctor because she felt male doctors didn't take a friend's illness seriously and led to the woman suffering pain more than she should have."

A frisson of uncomfortableness wormed its way up Johanna's spine. Richard was a quick one, and the first person who had ever come close to the truth of her reasons. Not even Faddil suspected her real need for obtaining a medical degree and a license to practice.

"Blackwell had a point." She stabbed the bite of soufflé. "Male doctors still don't take female or child patients half as seriously as they do male patients. I've seen too many missed diagnoses over the years."

"How many?" Richard appeared genuinely concerned.

"Isn't one too many?" She popped the bite into her mouth. It really was delicious. How wonderful it would be to return home from a hard day and have a hot meal ready and waiting for her.

She stabbed that train of thought with an imaginary fork. What was it about Richard Paine that had her daydreaming like a foolish schoolgirl? Did she really want a man to swoop in and save her?

No, she needed to take control. Richard could do his investigation from here tomorrow while she was at the hospital. Then she'd be done with him and could go on with her life.

Yet, the edge of her leather dress peeked from under the sheet lying in the corner of the living room. The memory of its message taunted her that this situation was far from over.

Chapter Seven

Rick expected Johanna to fight him much harder on the issue of accompanying her to the hospital. So, he wasn't a bit disappointed when she tried to sneak out of the flat at five a.m.

"Ready to go?" he asked cheerily from the dark breakfast nook as she tiptoed around the couch.

A little squeal came from her at the same moment she jumped. He rose and grabbed his thermos and the full carry cup he found in her cupboard last night.

"I have the tea, so I'm ready if you are." Part of him was glad she couldn't see his grin in the dark. And yet, his nerves sizzled at the thought of her punishing him. But he didn't dare ask what she would do. Doing so was too personal, too intimate. She'd kick him out in a heartbeat. His reasons for not wanting to leave had nothing to do with his honor or feelings of duty to protect her.

"You don't know how to take no for an answer, do you, Mister Paine?"

He expected her rancor, but she sounded more amused that he'd anticipated her attempt to evade him, rather than angry.

"You didn't say I couldn't go to the hospital with you," he replied. "You merely stated that you were annoyed by my insistence." He crossed to her and handed her the carry cup. "I'll drive."

"Parking will be terribly expensive," she said. However, she followed him out of the flat and locked the door behind her. The faint light of false dawn filtered through the hallway windows.

"Yes, it will." He didn't bother to mention the emir had advanced him two hundred pounds for incidental expenses. Both men knew exactly how Johanna would take that bit of information. "But I would be remiss in my duties if I allowed you to take public transportation right now."

She let out an exasperated sigh as they quietly treaded down the stairs.

When they stepped outside, shock ran through him. Under the streetlight, the cloth top of his convertible had been chopped into ribbons. All four tires had been slashed as well. And across the driver-side door white paint spelled "SLUT" across the deep blue lacquer.

The bastard harassing Johanna had just made this assignment personal.

Chapter Eight

Johanna winced as Rick swore vocally and at a high enough volume it woke Mrs. Cresswell and the new downstairs neighbor. She couldn't blame him for his rage. The same emotion had run through her when she saw what had been done to her favorite dress.

Monica, the new girl downstairs, held her calico cat tightly while Mrs. Cresswell muttered a few choice obscenities herself. A sense of déjà vu hit Johanna as she observed Monica, but she shook herself. She had probably glimpsed the girl while their landlady was showing her the downstairs flat.

"Shouldn't we call the police?" Monica asked hesitantly. "This is a terrible amount of damage for simple vandalism."

"No," Johanna said crisply.

"It's the '90's," the girl said. "No one's going to care if your boyfriend spent the night."

"I'm not her boyfriend," Richard ground out.

"I did my research." Monica stroked her cat, probably to comfort herself more than the animal. "I thought this was a safe neighborhood."

"It is, my dear," Mrs. Cresswell cooed. "It is. This is just an unfortunate incident. Why don't you go back inside and try to get some more sleep?"

Mrs. Cresswell wrapped an arm around Monica and guided the girl and the cat inside the house.

Johanna stared at the word scrawled in white paint on the side of Richard's convertible. This was definitely aimed at her, but she couldn't be responsible for any more injury to him.

"Perhaps it would be best if you went home," she murmured.

He cocked his head and stared at her. "In what?"

"I'll pay for a cab."

Richard opened his mouth to argue some more, but Mrs. Cresswell trotted out of the house with keys and a garage door opener in her hands.

"Take my vehicle, Mister Paine," the older woman ordered. "I have someone who can take care of your convertible while you guard my favorite tenant."

"But the top—" he started.

"It'll take a few days to order the cloth." She patted his arm. "Rest assured your convertible will be taken good care of. Consider it my gift for watching over Johanna."

Resentment flared inside Johanna. "I don't need to be watched over!"

"The slur on Mister Paine's automobile was not aimed at him," Mrs. Cresswell said primly.

"But he's only with me until two p.m.," Johanna protested.

"No, I'm staying until I catch this bastard," Rick snapped.

"That was not our agreement." Part of her wanted to stomp her foot, but doing so was little better than a toddler throwing a tantrum.

"Johanna, your stalker knew I spent the night in your apartment." Rick held up a hand when she opened her mouth. It irritated her to no end, but then, he was now a victim of her harasser also. She gestured for Rick to continue.

"Whatever fantasy he's conjured about you, he's now become dangerous." He waved toward his car. "He sees me as a threat, which means he'll redouble his efforts to finish this game his way."

"Does he really see this as a game?" she asked. It took phenomenal effort to keep her voice from trembling, but she managed.

"Yes." Rick frowned. His jaw muscle twitched as he obviously tried to find a way to formulate the situation so as not to scare her. That was an idiotic idea. She wasn't the type to frighten easily, but if her harasser was now targeting the people around her, she needed to think about her friends and co-workers.

"From the letters he sent you, he thinks he's wooing you," Rick said softly. He eyed Mrs. Cresswell who was doing her best to listen in. The landlady nodded in agreement.

"Is there someplace you can take Johanna?" Mrs. Cresswell asked. "Someplace this bastard can't find her."

"I don't know if that's a good idea." Rick frowned as he considered the problem. "He may decide to take his anger out on you and the other residents if she disappears."

"And if I don't keep to my normal schedule, we won't lure him into the open," Johanna said. "He's obviously keeping track of me somehow." She turned to Mrs. Cresswell. "Can you call a different locksmith? I'll pay for having the main door's locks changed."

"No, dear." Mrs. Cresswell lifted her chin. "I'm not taking another tuppence from you. I'm responsible for keeping my tenants safe."

Johanna clenched her jaw for a moment. She couldn't stand here and argue with her landlady, else she'd be late for her shift. "We'll discuss this when I get home. Tell the other girls—" She hesitated. Sharing her personal life wasn't something she did, but she didn't want to put the other two tenants in danger either.

"I'll tell them there was a break-in on top of the vandalism, and they need to stay with a friend for a couple of days until I get the locks changed." Mrs. Cresswell patted Johanna's arm. "Now, you two need to get going before you're late for your shift at the hospital."

"Thank you for your help." Johanna couldn't remember the last time someone was kind to her with no ulterior motive. The emotion lodged in her throat, and her eyes burned.

She turned and headed toward the gate to the garden and the garage behind the house. Her good feelings evaporated when the garage door gears started grinding. She thought she'd be rid of Richard Paine by late this afternoon. Now . . .

Now, she needed to find a way to get rid of him.

Before she did something very foolish to relieve her pent up emotions. Like kissing him.

Johanna glared at Richard as he guided Mrs. Cresswell's ancient Bentley through London's streets. He was rapidly becoming a thorn in her side.

"So, you are going to renege on our deal?" she snapped.

"Our deal was for me to give the emir twenty-four hours of my time free of charge to analyze the threat against you." He glanced at her before returning his attention to the road. "Your stalker has proven the threat is very real."

"How do I know you didn't sabotage your own vehicle in order to get Faddil's money?"

Tires screeched as Richard jerked the steering wheel to the left and into a parking space. They screeched again when he slammed on the brakes.

His gaze burned when he turned it on her. "How do I know you didn't pay someone to write those letters and vandalize my convertible to get back in the emir's good graces?"

Rage made spots dance in front of her eyes. "I would never! How dare you!"

Richard lowered his voice. "Now, you know how it feels to have your integrity impugned." He leaned back in the seat and blew out a deep breath. "Let's make a new deal. How about we stop casting aspersions about each other's character and deal with the problem at hand. The sooner we catch this bastard, the sooner we will be out of each other's hair."

Johanna stared out the windscreen, inhaled deeply, and released the air to calm herself. He was right. As much as she hated to admit it, Richard was correct. The person sending the letters and breaking into her flat was deeply disturbed. They needed to catch him before someone was injured.

Or worse.

She nodded before she looked at him again. "You're right. And I apologize for my behavior."

Richard inclined his head, but he said nothing more. Instead, he checked the automobile's mirrors before he pulled back into traffic.

Part of her was thankful for the silence the rest of the way to Tower Hospital. Why, oh, why couldn't she have met him at another time in her life? Richard had been a perfect gentleman, and here she was, taking her own fear out on him. And she could no longer fool herself. Not after the violent damage to his convertible.

Worry gnawed on her soul for the rest of the ride as she tried to ascertain who would want to scare her into submitting.

Better yet, why?

Chapter Nine

Rick parked Mrs. Cresswell's automobile in the employee's section of the hospital garage. Thankfully, Johanna's employee pass allowed admittance even though she admitted she regularly took the bus and the Tube to work.

Johanna marched through the side entrance and led him straight to Tower's security office. The department chief, a Mister Cunningham, raised his bushy white eyebrows when she informed him of the reason for Rick's presence.

"I don't know about allowing you in here, Mister Paine." Mister Cunningham scratched his fleshy jowl. "Have you cleared this through the hospital administrator?"

"Not yet," Rick said. "I was hired late yesterday afternoon. Doctor Ridgeley has been receiving threatening letters, which escalated to a break-in at her flat last night. No offence, but personal protection is not your responsibility. Nor would I want to impinge on you and your staff." He made a circling motion with his index finger. "I know what a maze this place can be, and there's too many spots the security cameras don't cover."

"All Mister Paine needs is a visitor's pass while I do my rounds," Johanna said. "He won't enter patients' room, just accompany me in the hallways until I can find Doctor Bennett and see what I need to do per hospital regulations."

"Very well." Mister Cunningham reached into his desk drawer and produced a visitor's card on a black lanyard. "But if anyone asks me, I'm going to tell them you were supposed to go straight to the administrator's office after you left here, Doctor Ridgeley."

She gave the security chief a brilliant smile. "Thank you very much for your assistance, Mister Cunningham. I greatly appreciate it."

For a brief instant, jealousy reared its ugly head in Rick's soul. He'd do just about anything for Johanna to bestow one of those smiles on him. He quickly smote his little green-eyed monster. He needed to keep his head on straight. Catching the bastard harassing her should be his top priority. Not mooning over his charge.

"What now?" Rick asked as they exited the security office.

"I find Doctor Bennett like I said I would." She set off at a brisk pace toward the elevators. "Then, I need to stow my belongings and get started on my rounds."

However, things with Johanna's supervisor did not go as well as she assumed.

"No," Doctor Bennett bit out. "I won't allow a stranger free access through my ward."

"But, sir—" Johanna started.

"What part of no did you not understand, Doctor Ridgeley?" He glared at her over the rims of his reading glasses.

"Thank you for your input, Doctor." Rick watched Bennett carefully. "You've just been moved to the top of my suspect list."

"Now, just a minute here—" Bennett stood as he spoke.

"Doctor Ridgeley, would you mind giving us a moment of privacy?" Rick crossed imaginary fingers she would pick up on why without him having to spell it out.

Her perturbed expression faded, and she nodded. "I'll be outside."

She pivoted smoothly on her heel and stalked out of Bennett's office, closing the door behind her.

"I don't appreciate being threatened," Bennett snapped.

"Do you think the Royal College of Physicians would appreciate you hitting on your female interns?" Rick replied.

Bennet's face paled, and he slowly sat down. "What do you want? Money?"

"This isn't about money." Rick leaned his palms on Bennett's desk. "Where were you yesterday between eleven a.m. and three p.m.?"

Bennett blinked slowly. "You're serious."

"As a corpse."

"I was here at the hospital the entire time," Bennett protested. "I didn't break into Johanna's flat."

"That is Doctor Ridgeley to you from now on," Rick snapped while he pulled out his pad and pen. ""Who can verify your whereabouts?"

"The head nurse of the oncology department and the three senior house officers on duty yesterday." Bennett's cheeks reddened.

"Let me guess," Rick said sarcastically. "One of the SHOs was the other female student reporting to you?"

Bennett said nothing, but his ears turned a peculiar shade of purple.

"Here's the deal." Rick replaced his notebook and pen in his jacket pocket. "You will drop your relationship with the other woman, and I won't tell any of Johanna's very powerful friends you were the one threatening her."

"P-powerful f-friends?" Bennett licked his lips.

"You know what a mere SHO makes. Johanna cannot afford my rates," Rick said with a smile. "However, the gentlemen who are paying me are not happy about this situation. Do we have an agreement?"

Bennett nodded.

Good. Rick turned and left the office. Maybe the wanker would leave the rest of the female physicians alone. Doubtful it will last for long, but one could hope.

He found Johanna chatting with another woman at the nurse's station. The doctor wrapped her arm around the distraught lady. He stayed back until the teary-eyed stranger left.

"Is everything all right?" he asked as he approached Johanna.

"No, not exactly." She beckoned him to follow her. "Did you end up threatening Doctor Bennett?"

"Yes."

She stopped, whirled, and gaped at him. "You what?"

"Do you really think you were the only woman the bastard has been hitting on?" Rick shook his head. "My guess is his side pieces are the real reason for his divorce."

Johanna's shoulders sagged. "I should have known."

"You can't blame yourself for Bennett being a wanker," Rick protested. He wanted to wipe that sad expression off her beautiful face.

"No, it's that—" She pursed her lips. "My other relationships are much more honest than the vanilla ones, whether I accept the men's proposals or not." She looked up at him. "Does that make any sense?"

"Yes, it does." He regarded her, hoping she would take his next words in the spirit that he meant. "To properly serve, one must open up their soul. To trust the other person whole-heartedly, and to offer the same honesty in return."

"Does anyone know the truth about you?" she asked softly.

"Just Jamie." Rick shrugged. "It's probably why he really contacted me. He knew I wouldn't be bothered by the relationship between you and the emir."

They continued walking down the hall.

"Yet, the minister didn't tell you prior to your arrival at Faddil's hotel," she murmured.

"No, he didn't, but I'm fairly certain it was more for yours and the emir's protection than to throw me under the bus." Rick smiled at her once again.

They reached the locker room for the female doctors.

"This is the only entrance or exit?" he asked.

"I don't plan on escaping you through the loo," she said with impudent grin.

"That's good," he said with mock seriousness. "I wouldn't like to ruin my one good suit by swimming through the sewer after you."

Johanna shook her head and chuckled as she pushed the door open. She had a very nice laugh when she let it out, but then, she didn't have much to laugh about over the last eighteen hours. Part of him was pleased he could bring that side out of her in such dire circumstances.

A scream rang out, and Rick barged through the swinging door, propriety be damned.

No one was in the lounge area. Rick charged through the doorway leading to the lockers.

"Johanna!"

"Back here!" Anger filled her voice.

Rick darted to the left and found her in the last row. Her hands were clenched as she stared inside her locker. He reached her, but the rancid smell drew his attention.

Inside the locker was a dead rat, pinned to a board with its chest and abdomen cut open as if someone practiced an autopsy on the animal.

Chapter Ten

"I should have listened to you yesterday." Johanna looked up at Rick. "I owe you an apology."

"Are you all right?"

She swallowed hard. "I'm fine. It . . . startled me." She held up her padlock. "I swear I locked it when I left Monday, and it was still locked when I came in here a minute ago."

"It looks like someone performed an autopsy on it," he commented.

"Whoever it was also left another note." She pointed to the white envelope taped to her locker door. Instead of her name and address this time, "Beloved J" was scrawled in what looked to be blood on the face of the envelope.

The loud crash came from the lounge before Mister Cunningham charged around the bank of lockers.

"One of the nurses reported screaming—" he started before he wrinkled his nose. "What the devil is that smell?"

Both she and Rick stepped aside so the security chief could see inside her locker.

"For the love of—"

"Is everything all right back there, Mr. Cunningham?" a female voice called out.

"Someone playing a damn foolish joke on one of the doctor's, Miss Huxley," he said.

When the woman came around the corner, she wore a nurse's uniform, but it was her familiar face that shocked Johanna. "Monica?"

A shy smile graced her neighbor's face. "Hello again, Johanna." Her expression quickly fell, and her nose wrinkled. "Did someone leave their lunch in here over the weekend?"

"It's a dead rat—" Mr. Cunningham started.

Johanna pulled the door partially shut so as not to alarm the girl. "It must have wormed its way into my locker, then got stuck while I was off for the last two days."

"Oh, the poor thing!" Monica clasped her hands together. "I heard the scream, and—"

"I was simply startled. Why don't you go about your duties?" Johanna smiled. "I have two big strapping men to help me deal with the rat. But thank you for calling for help, Nurse Huxley."

"I guess we do need to mind our 'p's and 'q's while at the hospital," Monica said.

Johanna suppressed a wince. Had she accidentally hurt the girl's feelings? That was definitely not a good way to cement a neighborly relationship.

"Only at the hospital," Johanna assured her. Monica nodded and left the locker area.

"Maybe we should call the bobbies," Mister Cunningham said after the outer door wheezed shut. "If someone's harassing you with these mean tricks—"

"And tell the police what?" Johanna waved at the dead rat. "Did this actually threaten my life?"

"I need to check the letter," Rick said. "Do you have some rubber gloves around here?"

Mister Cunningham nodded. "I'll fetch you a box."

Once he left, Johanna eyed Rick. "I think this goes to show the culprit is someone at the hospital trying to get me to quit."

He shook his head. "Honestly, it wouldn't be that hard to sneak in here." He gestured toward the corridor. "There's blind spots the cameras don't cover. All I'd need is a lab coat. I'd keep my head down. Come in here between shifts. Your padlock is a standard one from a hardware shop. It would be easy to pick."

"Is that what you were doing last night while I was asleep?" she huffed. "Plotting on how to extend your interference in my life?"

"No, I'm trying to think like your stalker if I want to get a step ahead of him," Rick retorted. The pensive look on his face eased. "You said you hadn't met Nurse Huxley when she moved into the first floor flat?"

"I didn't." Johanna shrugged. "I didn't even know she worked here until a few minutes ago." She stared at the ceiling, trying not to breathe too deeply. "That could be why she seemed familiar this morning. I must have glimpsed her here."

"I take it from your conversation the doctors and nurses don't mix?"

She shook her head. "The hospital administrator is quite adamant about proper protocols. It's the reason I turned down Doctor Bennett. I wasn't joking about us being fired."

"Do those protocols apply to hospital staff living in the same building?" Rick asked.

"Probably." Johanna bit her lip. "But I'm not going to be mean to Monica just because she's a nurse if that's what you're asking."

"Actually, I haven't seen you be anything other than polite to everyone from a world leader to the lowest level of staff here at Tower." He smiled at her.

For some reason, his observation triggered a tickle of warmth inside her. Most men took civility as a sign of weakness. To her, it was a strength. She often learned a great deal of information simply by being polite. But that politeness would drop the instant someone tried to hurt her or someone she loved.

As her mother's physician had found out years ago.

"So what do you plan to do with that?" She pointed at the rat.

"Well, you and the emir wanted discretion." He frowned at the dead animal. "Any suggestions on how to discreetly take it home with us?"

Johanna closed her eyes. This was going to be a very long day indeed.

Thankfully, she had a clean jacket in her bag since everything in her locker smelled like dead rat. Rick promised to clean up the mess and deodorize her locker. Even he pointed out there was little chance her harasser could do anything to her directly while she was in the company of the other SHOs during morning rounds.

Despite her efforts to be early, Johanna was still five minutes late. She and the other four SHO's tensed, expecting Doctor Bennett to inflict a sharp lecture on tardiness. He merely frowned and said, "Try to be on time in the future, Doctor Ridgeley."

The other students eyed her with varying degrees of resentment and curiosity.

"Yes, sir," she replied crisply. What had Rick privately said to her supervisor? The last thing she needed was special treatment. She'd tried so hard to fit in here. Act like any other vanilla physician.

She tried to ignore the odd looks from her peers and focused on the patients. Thankfully, the morning whizzed by in a blur of activity. When they broke for lunch, the only other female SHO Doctor Oakes approached her.

"Want to join me in the cafeteria to review our notes?"

"I'd love to—" Johanna started. Rick waved at her from the nurses' station. "Unfortunately, there's a personal matter I need to attend to."

Oakes stepped closer and lowered her voice. "Does it have to do with the dead rat some wanker left in your locker?"

Johanna stared at Oakes. "How did you hear about that?"

Oakes shrugged. "The nurse grapevine." She grinned. "They forget there are physicians in the ladies' lavatory these days."

Johanna frowned. "What exactly are they saying?"

"It's a toss up between whether I did it to drive you out of Tower in a jealous rage, or whether Bennett did it because you turned him down."

"Why on earth would you be jealous of me?" Johanna asked.

"That's the other rumor. Allegedly, I am sleeping with Bennett to further my career." Oakes chuckled.

"You're not, are you?"

"Heavens, no! I'm not that thick." Oakes laughed even louder before she looked around and whispered. "He's been shagging a few of the nurses."

"More than one? At the same time?" Johanna tried to wear the appropriate appalled expression though she'd witnessed much more intricate and salacious maneuvers at Club Noir.

Oakes snickered. "One at a time I believe. I only caught the one. Don't know who it was because I only saw her back, but her panties fell out of the leg of her scrubs when she exited Bennett's office.

"They could have simply been caught in her scrubs with static from the clothes dryer," Johanna protested.

"Then they would have been clean," Oakes whispered.

Rick approached them, and Oakes gave him a frank appraisal. Jealousy reared its ugly head in the back of Johanna's mind. Why on earth would she care if another woman found Rick attractive? She didn't have the time for a relationship.

Right?

"Doctor Ridgeley, when you're finished here, we need to speak," he said.

Oakes grinned again. "I can see why you're passing on lunch with me. I don't blame you one bit." She held out her right hand to Rick. "Laurel Oakes."

He took the proffered palm and shook it. "Rick Paine."

"I wouldn't advertise that name around here. The staff will think you're hitting us up for narcotics." Oakes laughed at her bad joke and waved. "Catch you during the afternoon session, Ridgeley."

"What was that all about?" Rick murmured.

Johanna's stomach rumbled, reminding her she hadn't eaten anything since last night. "Let's stop by the cafeteria, then eat on the back patio while we'll compare notes. The last thing I need is to faint from hunger during my afternoon duties."

Chapter Eleven

Rick chewed his rather tasteless sandwich while Johanna relayed what she learned from Doctor Oakes.

When she finished, he said, "Are you sure she's not covering up her tracks?"

"I don't believe so, but it's not like we are more than colleagues." Johanna shrugged and sipped water from her bottle. "Did you ask Bennett when you spoke to him privately this morning?"

"He's definitely shagging someone here from his reaction, but no, I didn't ask him directly." He wadded up the wrappings, leaned over, and tossed the garbage in the nearby bin. "That voice on the phone yesterday definitely sounded male, but maybe it was Bennett's sidepiece. Maybe she discovered he was interested in you and doesn't want the competition. Maybe she got a brother to call you or another chum."

Johanna frowned. "That's a lot of supposition packed in your paragraph."

"I know." The entire situation was an itch he couldn't reach. Or in the case of Johanna herself, shouldn't reach.

"What about the note my rat killer left?"

Today's note was the last thing he wanted to discuss. Especially with Johanna. Especially after the entire damn missive had been written in blood. Probably the poor rat's.

"It's pretty much the same as the rest of your letters," he said.

She regarded him for a long time before she murmured, "I thought we were past lying to each other, Rick."

It was the first time he heard his nickname from her lips. And that little sound sent an intimate thrill through him, though nothing could come of his attraction to her. She'd made it clear her career was her focus right now.

"You're right." He leaned his elbows on the table. "It's obvious your stalker left the note and the rat before I got involved in your case. This missive states he plans to do something to get your attention while you are at the hospital."

Johanna's expression grew pensive. "You mean the rat?"

Rick shook his head. "He mentions dressing you up like the queen you are, how much he likes your black leather dress, and compares you to Marie Antoinette."

She drew back. "Marie Antoinette was sent to the guillotine."

"Your stalker didn't know you had lunch planned with the emir yesterday." Rick hesitated a moment. "It was probably a good thing you weren't home."

"I didn't know I was having lunch with Faddil until yesterday morning." Johanna's frown deepened. "There was a last minute cancellation in his schedule. Only his staff—" Her eyes widened. "No. No, that can't be."

"Maybe because he misses you?" Rick ventured.

"It would be a good reason for his staff to target me." She shook her head. "No, none of this makes sense. If Hosni or one of the other bodyguards wanted me out of the way, there's a million other ways to keep me from Faddil."

"A million?" Rick didn't like his suspicion. "Is that your price?"

An icy expression fell over her face. "No. I meant they could have simply disappeared me. No one gives a damn when women disappear. I would have been just another unsolved missing persons case."

"I would give a damn," Rick snapped. "And I think the emir would too, which is why you wouldn't simply disappear." He tried to expel his anger with the air in his lungs. "This letter was very personal. Whoever sent it mentioned your dress, as if he had seen you wear it before. When was the last time you wore it?"

Johanna rested her chin on her palm. "It was to Club Noir. About two years ago during the Christmas initiations the year before last."

"That was the last time you were at the club, right?"

She nodded.

"I'm sorry I never got to see you in it." The words popped out of Rick's mouth before he could stop them. He had no right to say them, especially to Johanna. Not when he was supposed to be protecting her.

Something subtle changed in her expression.

"Forget I said that," he muttered.

"I can't," she murmured. "Is that the real reason you insist on remaining by my side? You're attracted to me?"

Something told him if he lied now, she'd kick him to the curb. Without someone to watch her back, she'd be in even more danger. But telling her the truth might destroy any chance of seeing her once he caught the stalker.

"I am attracted to you, but my duty to your safety needs to come first." He looked down at his hands, trying to find the right words to say. "If we'd met at another time, I would want to serve you as you deserved to be served." He met her gaze again. "But this isn't the right time."

"No, it isn't." Was that regret that passed across her face? Johanna took another sip of her water. "I need to get back—" She waved toward the entrance to the cafeteria.

He nodded and collected the wrapper from her sandwich. They both rose from their chairs, and he tossed the garbage into the bin.

"I know you're not going to like the idea, but what if we find somewhere else for you to stay while I check alibis for our suspects over the last couple of days?" he said as they walked back into the cafeteria.

"You're right," she said. "I don't like it."

"Doctor Ridgeley, if this person's actions escalate—"

"I promise I'll take your suggestion under advisement, Mister Paine." Except the way she curled his family name sent a wave of anticipation through him. Maybe his admission and promise to behave had softened her attitude toward him.

"That's all I ask," he murmured.

"Thank you for asking." She smiled at him.

If that bright smile was all he could have from her, then he'd take it.

The rest of the afternoon passed uneventfully. Rick made phone calls concerning the other people on Johanna's list, but he couldn't seem to get any solid information. The locksmith Mrs. Cresswell used was licensed and had a solid reputation in the trade, but that didn't mean the gentleman or one of his employees hadn't gone crackers.

Security Chief Cunningham finagled the head of the morgue into letting Rick keep the dead rat in one of their body coolers until Johanna's shift was over. The man was even good enough to find a disposable cooler and ice for the evidence during the ride home.

Other than Johanna insisting they stop and fill the petrol tank on Mrs. Cresswell's vehicle on the way home, the evening's ride back to Johanna's flat seemed almost . . . domestic. They discussed the odds of the prime minister keeping her coalition together, whether their favorite teams would win the English football title, and how much they both hated the influx of American fast food restaurants.

Rick pulled into the alley and opened the garage door. Once he parked, he and Johanna collected their things, including the damn rat. Any other woman he know would have thrown a fit. However, she was the one who pointed out his forethought on bringing his investigative tools and his go bag into the flat so they weren't damaged when her stalker vandalized his car.

Johanna pulled her keys from her purse. When she touched the knob on the back door of the old house, the door swung. She glanced at him, but she said nothing. Instead, she stepped out of the way. Her silent gesture said this door was normally locked.

He set the cooler containing the white board and the dead rat on a nearby bench before he pushed the door open a little wider. He winced at the squeak of the hinges and stepped inside. Silence reigned inside the huge Georgian monstrosity. With the sun on the west side of the building, the hallway was dim.

Though he tried to tread silently down the hallway, the antique floorboards creaked beneath his soles. The stair steps to the second floor also announced his presence. The entrance to both Johanna's flat and the one next door had notes taped on them. Mrs. Cresswell's flowing handwriting said for the girls to come see her for the new keys. Johanna's flat was securely locked, as was Felicity's across the hall. He tore off the note on Johanna's door and headed back downstairs.

Johanna still waited outside the house. Part of him was gratified she wasn't disregarding his precautions anymore like the American singer he'd babysat last year. That git was lucky she was still alive.

"Mrs. Cresswell changed the locks like she promised." Rick handed the piece of paper to Johanna.

A wry smile crossed her face as she perused the note. "So my keys wouldn't have worked anyway." She shook her head and looked up at him. "I do hope she didn't leave the back door unlocked because of me. That wasn't a wise move."

"Let's collect your new keys, and you can scold Mrs. Cresswell at your leisure." He grinned back at her.

Johanna charged into the house while he collected his cooler of possible evidence. She knocked on Mrs. Cresswell's door for the second time when he caught up to her.

"Could she have stepped out for the evening?" Rick asked.

Johanna frowned. "That would have left me and the other tenants locked out. She wouldn't have done that." She rattled the knob, and the door opened.

Alarm raced through Rick's blood when they both stepped inside. Silver white hair stained in red stuck out from behind one of Mrs. Cresswell's period-correct club chairs.

Chapter Twelve

This time, Johanna didn't have a choice about talking to the police. Officers took both hers and Rick's statements on the front walk while the paramedics tended to Mrs. Cresswell inside her flat. She told them about the open back door and the changing of the locks.

"Why did she change the locks today?"

"Someone broke into my flat yesterday," she replied.

The officer cocked his head. "Did you report this?"

"No," she said. "Nothing was stolen. The only damage was to one of my dresses."

The officer inclined his head toward Rick. "Who's that guy? Your boyfriend?"

"No, he's a security consultant." She glanced at Rick. "I've been receiving some odd letters. An acquaintance of mine recommended him."

"And who was this acquaintance?"

No, she couldn't bring up Faddil's name. This mess could accidentally end up in one of the rags. "M.P. James Henry Wynton-Smythe," she murmured.

The officer's right eyebrow rose. "You need to be honest, Miss Ridgeley—"

She narrowed her eyes. "That is Doctor Ridgeley."

"Are you more than acquaintances with Minister Wynton-Smythe,

Doctor Ridgeley?" He bit out her title in such a condescending way part of her wanted to slap him.

"No, we are not."

"The minister does have a certain reputation—"

"I don't sleep with married men," she snapped. Her fists clenched of her own accord. This was exactly why she didn't mention Faddil. "And I don't appreciate you casting aspersions when my landlady is lying on the floor of her flat and seriously injured!"

"Have any of the other tenants reported a break-in?" he asked. At least, he quit his previous line of questions.

"Not to my knowledge," she said crisply. "Mrs. Cresswell planned to change all the locks to our flats and the main front and back doors just to be safe."

"Did you treat the victim?"

"As best as I could," Johanna ground out. "I made sure her heart was beating and her airway wasn't obstructed. After that, I applied pressure to the head wound to slow the bleeding until the emergency personnel arrived."

"Are you her personal physician?"

"No, I merely rendered first aid considering the circumstances," Johanna replied. Now, where on earth was the officer going with this?

"What about your security consultant?" The officer's tone indicated how poorly he thought of Rick's status.

"He told me not to touch anything that I didn't have to," Johanna said. Irritation danced in her voice, and she couldn't stop it. "To preserve the crime scene for you lot. Then he grabbed the envelope on Mrs. Cresswell's side table with my name on it and the new keys inside. He ran up to my flat to call the authorities."

The police jotted down her words and snapped his notebook shut. "If a detective has any other questions, he'll contact you." He stalked off.

Rick joined her. "Thank you for not striking the policeman," he murmured.

"Was I that obvious?" she asked quietly. However, her attention was solely on the pale face of Mrs. Cresswell as the paramedics rolled the gurney out of the house and loaded her into the back of the ambulance.

"Johanna!"

They both turned in the direction of the voice. Monica ran up to them and breathlessly asked, "What happened?" Her alarmed attention was on the ambulance while it pulled away, its siren blaring.

"Mrs. Cresswell was attacked," Johanna said.

"What? How?" Monica blinked as she obviously tried to process the information. "She told me this morning she was changing the locks because someone broke into your flat yesterday and then your friend's car was vandalized."

As much as Johanna disliked her personal business becoming a subject of gossip, Mrs. Cresswell did the right thing. She would want to make sure both Monica and Felicity were safe. However, this whole problem was rapidly spinning out of control.

"Here's your keys." Johanna slipped the envelope from her purse and handed it to Monica. She'd grabbed the other two envelopes before the police arrived at the house.

Monica took the envelope and stared at it a moment before she looked up at Johanna. "What if whoever hurt Mrs. Cresswell has copies of all our keys now?"

"Do you have someplace you can stay for tonight?" Rick asked. "A friend or family member? If you don't feel safe, you should always trust your instincts."

"Yes, I do." A tremulous smile graced Monica's face. "Thank you for watching out for us."

Once again, jealousy tainted Johanna's emotions. Was it Rick's admission of his feelings at lunch? Or had she simply not been with a man for so long the need had become an itch even her vibrator couldn't relieve?

Unfortunately, the same police officer who had interviewed her stalked back to their little group. "Do you live here, miss?" he snapped at Monica.

The nurse trembled at his aggressive behavior. "Yes."

"Please step over here." He motioned. "I need to ask you some questions."

Monica shot a scared look at Johanna before she said, "Am I in trouble?"

"No, you're not." Johanna glared at the officer. "He's gathering information about all of us."

"B-but I was working at the hospital," Monica choked out. "You saw me there!"

"Don't worry." Johanna wrapped her arm around the younger woman. "A couple of dozen people can verify where we were when the attack occurred. But you might have noticed something you don't realize is important, which is why the officers need to question all of us."

"Very well, then." Monica nodded. She and the policeman moved out of earshot.

Johanna looked up at Rick. "What do we do now? I don't have Felicity's office number, and I doubt if the police are going to let us back into Mrs. Cresswell's flat to look for it."

"No, they're not," Rick said grimly.

A terrible thought occurred as police officers rounded the building to search the garden and garage. "What did you do with the damn rat?"

His rueful smile was endearing and scary at the same time. "It's sitting in your practically empty refrigerator."

After the police departed and she left her own note on Felicity's door, Johanna walked with Rick and Monica down to the bus stop. The setting sun cast long shadows across the city, and for the first time in her life, Johanna was truly frightened by what those shadows might be hiding.

Once Monica boarded the bus to her friend's house, Johanna and Rick strolled down to the neighborhood fish and chips kiosk. The crisp smell of fried food had her stomach rumbling by the time they arrived.

She slapped Rick's hand when he reached for his wallet. "You don't pay."

Surprisingly, Rick said nothing more than "Yes, ma'am."

The proprietor, however, snickered as he made the change and handed her their food. Grease already seeped through the paper sack.

"May I carry it?" Rick asked when they were far enough the proprietor couldn't overhear them.

"Yes, you may." She handed him the bag. He tried awfully hard to be deferential and appropriately respectful when her safety wasn't on the line. Surely, she could reciprocate.

"Do you still suspect the old locksmith?" she asked. "Mrs. Cresswell wouldn't have reneged on her word to you to hire someone else."

"And therein lies the problem." Rick frowned as he check for vehicles before they crossed the street. "We have the name of the second locksmith, but their shop doesn't open again until the morning."

"Something else is bothering you though," Johanna said.

"We were awfully loud when we discovered the damage to my convertible this morning. In fact, we woke up Mrs. Cresswell and Monica, but not Felicity."

"If she sleeps in the bedroom overlooking the garden like I do, I doubt she would have heard us."

"What about Mrs. Cresswell and Monica?" he asked.

"The fireplaces still exist in the front corner rooms. Mrs. Cresswell sleeps there for the extra heat in the winter." Johanna considered what little she knew about her new neighbor. "Perhaps Monica sleeps in the front bedroom as well."

"Possibly," Rick mused. "I need to ask her tomorrow."

"What else are you thinking?" Johanna prodded.

"How do you know?" Rick glanced at her. "You've only known me for a day."

"The same way you know and understand me," she said. A little courtesy could go a long way. "Please tell me what you're thinking."

"What if your stalker is a neighbor in one of the other houses on the street?" The streetlight blinked on and illuminated his frown as they walked. "If he heard Mrs. Cresswell say she was calling another locksmith, he might have pretended to be the locksmith."

"But the locks were changed," she protested.

Rick looked down at her. "Doctor Ridgeley, I can change a bloody lock. It wouldn't be that hard to grab a few business cards and pretend to be the locksmith."

"But what about the real locksmith?" Johanna wasn't quite sure where Rick was going, but she already didn't like it.

"He could have rang the actual locksmith and cancelled the call."

"That pretty much takes us back to square one," she muttered.

"I know."

She pulled her keys from her purse as they approached the old Georgian. "Some food and a good night's sleep should clear our minds."

"Would you mind if I try something since I seem to enrage your stalker?" he asked.

Johanna paused in twisting the door knob and looked up at him. "Of course not."

His head lowered, and his lips touched her. The kiss was gentle. Sweet even. No pushing for more as men often had the tendency to do.

She reached up and cupped the back of his neck, urging him to do a more thorough job, but he broke their contact.

"That should be sufficient," he murmured.

No. No, that one kiss would never be sufficient. Her determination not to make Rick Paine hers shattered like the walls of Jericho.

Chapter Thirteen

Rick expected Johanna to slap him. Yell at him. Any reaction to overstepping her bounds even if it were for a good cause.

Instead, she remained silent, but some sort of resolve lay in her expression. One that sent a wave of need through him.

She turned the knob and stepped inside the old Georgian house, flipping on the main hallway lights as she entered. Police tape marked the door to Mrs. Cresswell's apartment in a huge colorful "X". She hesitated for a moment before she resolutely marched up the stairs.

Once again, she unlocked the door, pushed it open, and turned on the living room lights. Rick breathed a little sigh of relief that everything was still as they left it this morning. He carried the sack over to Johanna's little table while she locked the door behind them.

The phone jangled, and he couldn't miss Johanna jumping at the noise. He motioned he'd pick up the other receiver in her bedroom. She nodded, and he raced into the other room.

"Hello?" Johanna's normal self-confidence showed in her voice. Good. Maybe she'd keep her head long enough for them to learn something more about her stalker.

Rick eased the receiver from its cradle and gently released the button to connect to the call.

"Johanna? This is Felicity from next door," the feminine voice said.

He relaxed a fraction. It definitely wasn't the same person who called Johanna yesterday.

"Felicity! I have the new keys to your flat," Johanna said.

"That's what the locksmith said." Felicity sighed in obvious relief. "I'm at the Golden Boar. I'll be at the front door in five minutes."

"When did you speak—" Johanna said, but the other woman had already hung up.

Rick returned the receiver to its cradle and stalked back into the living room. "We can question her when she arrives."

"You don't think she . . ."

He shook his head. "I don't know. Your stalker could have fooled her just like he did Mrs. Cresswell."

"Do you think Mrs. Cresswell became suspicious, and that's why he attacked her?"

As much as he wanted to protect Johanna's feelings, he'd promised not to lie to her. "That's exactly my question. Mrs. Cresswell doesn't seem the type for subterfuge. If he said or did something that gave him away, I doubt she could have hid her feelings. But we're not going to know until she regains consciousness."

Johanna looked longingly at the sack on the table. "We've got enough food for three. What if we invite Felicity to join us for dinner?"

Her suggestion wasn't what he really wanted, but it was the smarter choice. If Johanna's stalker had spoken with the solicitor from the flat across the hallway, she could probably give them a decent description of the bastard.

"Oh, thank you so much for dinner," Felicity said as she crammed another large bite of fish in her mouth. "I missed lunch. You're lucky. Your patients don't scream at you when they do something stupid, then expect you to skip meals and fix it for them." Other than the chunks of blond hair amidst dark auburn locks, Johanna's next door neighbor was rather average looking.

At least, compared to Johanna.

"Oh, you'd change your opinion after a day in an ER rotation." Johanna chuckled.

"We admit we have an ulterior movement for bribing you with food," Rick admitted.

Felicity's eyes widened. She set down her piece of fish and licked her fingers before wiping them with a napkin. "A threesome?" She shrugged. "I'm game. It's been a hell of a week at the office. I could use the stress relief." She reached for the top button of her blouse.

"No!" Rick cleared his throat before he added more calmly, "Nothing like that. I have some questions about your encounter with the locksmith this evening."

"Oh, him." Felicity waved her fingers. "Not as much fun, but fire away."

Rick flipped open his notebook. "Can you give me a description of him?"

"You think he's the one who assaulted Mrs. Cresswell?" Felicity popped a chip into her mouth.

"Possibly," Rick admitted.

Felicity swallowed her mouthful of fried potato. "Then I should be giving this statement to the police, not you."

"I hired Rick as my personal security consultant," Johanna interjected. "This all seemed to start when I received some letters last month that have grown progressively more threatening."

Felicity took a swig from her bottle of lager. The pack of beer was her contribution to the dinner. She leaned back in her chair, scowled, and shook her head. "I don't get why exes can't seem to grasp the concept of the word 'no.'"

"What do you mean?" Rick asked.

"I've been involved in too many divorces where the husbands think their wives are personal property." She picked at the label on her bottle. "I've seen a number of clients killed by these assholes." She turned her attention to Johanna. "Let me guess. Ex-boyfriend?"

"That's what we're trying to find out," Johanna said evenly. "I haven't been seeing anyone for the last couple of years."

"Oh, believe me. I know." Felicity grinned. "You've been grumpier than a football fan after their team lost a game. And Mrs. Cresswell says there's been a distinct lack of noise coming from your flat."

"What?" Johanna looked . . . well horrified wasn't quite the word, but she definitely didn't like people knowing her private business.

"Don't fret, Johanna." Felicity giggled. "I stayed in Mrs. Cresswell's spare bedroom one night when one of my own ex-boyfriends threw a rock through my window. Isaac boarded it up until it could be replaced, but it was that night we actually had ice, and Mrs. Cresswell was worried about me getting sick from the cold."

Felicity's expression fell. "It was easier to let her take care of me than to argue with her. I do hope she'll be all right."

"I promise I'll go into the hospital early tomorrow and check on her," Johanna said.

"About the man you saw here this evening?" Rick prompted. He tried not to let his aggravation at the conversation's swerve show. It was foolish to think Johanna had never dated or had sex, but he really didn't want to know the details.

Felicity took a deep breath and stared at the ceiling. "Roughly one and three-quarter meters, thirteen stone. His hair was dark brown. No facial hair. Bit of an East End accent. He was dressed in dark blue trousers and a light blue shirt with a cap stating his company." She looked at Rick again. "I'm sorry. I don't remember the company's name."

"Then it couldn't be Isaac," Johanna blurted. "He's blond."

"You ladies know how easy it is to change the color of one's hair," Rick remarked.

"I think Mrs. Cresswell would recognize her own nephew," Johanna said dryly.

Rick faced Felicity again. "Did he give you a card?"

Felicity shook her head. "He wrote Johanna's number on a blank sheet of paper from his clipboard and gave it to me. When I asked him if he could just let me in, he said it was against company policy. He insisted she had the new keys to my flat, and she would be home momentarily."

Johanna stared at Rick. "How did he know?"

"You left the note on Felicity's door, remember?" But he spoke with no humor in his voice. Johanna was not a woman one laughed at and emerge unscathed. Not that the situation was one bit funny.

"Do you have a friend you can stay with, Felicity?" Johanna murmured. "Monica downstairs is staying with a friend tonight after the attack on Mrs. Cresswell."

Felicity sighed. "I'll pack a bag and head to my sister's. I don't relish sleeping on her couch, but I would like it even less if someone assaulted me in my sleep."

"We can give you a ride," Johanna offered.

"If it's not too much trouble." Felicity waved her hand nonchalantly. "I just need to get to the nearest Tube station." She grabbed the last bite of her fish. "Give me five minutes to get what I'll need for an overnight stay and give my sister a ring to warn her of my impending arrival." She popped the morsel into her mouth, grabbed her purse, and sauntered out of Johanna's flat.

Rick turned to Johanna. "What's the Golden Boar?"

"It's the neighborhood pub. Two blocks away." Johanna pointed in the opposite direction of the fish and chips kiosk.

"I'm up for a pint tonight after we drop off Felicity at the Tube station. Why don't you join me?"

"Do I have a choice?" She smirked at him.

"Depends on if you want to end up like the damn rat inside your refrigerator," he commented.

Johanna dropped her argument.

Chapter Fourteen

Johanna looked around the Golden Boar. Dark wood dominated the open space. In the corner, a group of four men laughed and insulted each other as they played darts. The scent of thick brewer's yeast mixed with the hearty odor of beef.

She used to come in here with some fellow students while in medical school. It had been so long she thought no one would recognize her. But Lachlan still stood behind the bar. And he had helped relieve her stress before exams and papers more than once.

He waved. "Doctor Jo! It's been a while."

"Someone you know," Rick murmured.

"Used to," she replied while she waved back.

Lachlan finished drawing a couple of pints for the two men at the bar. His sandy blond hair stood out at wild angles as it had two years ago. The baby softness of his features from before had shifted to an angled cheek and jaw. He was simply on of those men who would get better looking as he aged.

Lachlan shifted to Johanna and Rick's end of the bar as they approached. "What can I get for you and your friend, Doctor Jo?"

"Two pints of Irish red, and the answers to a few questions," Johanna replied.

Lachlan's cocky grin lit up the pub. "Two pints I can handle, but I thought you knew all the answers, Doctor Jo." He turned to grab a couple of mugs from the shelf.

"What does he mean you know all the answers?" Rick murmured.

She closed her eyes and sucked in a deep breath. Damn men and their huge egos. Of course, Rick looked at Lachlan as competition, even though things had never really started between her and the bartender.

"Ah," Rick breathed. "He was the loud sex the night Felicity spent with Mrs. Cresswell."

"If you must know, yes," she hissed.

"And you're worried I'll put him on my suspect list?"

She opened her eyes and glared at Rick. "Aren't you?"

He shrugged. "It depends on how things go with his answers."

Lachlan placed the two pints with dark red beer in front of them. Johanna handed him enough bills for the pints and a healthy gratuity.

"One of my flatmates Felicity was here earlier this evening," Johanna began. "She has auburn hair with blond chunks—"

Lachlan held up his palm. "She was here, whinging that her landlady changed the locks to her building without warning. So she did get a hold of you?"

"Yes, she did—"

"Was she here with anyone?" Rick interrupted.

Lachlan chuckled and leaned his elbows on the bar's surface. "Not for lack of trying on her part while she downed her lager. You aren't her man, are you?"

"No," Rick said, abruptly enough even Johanna had to laugh. "We're wondering if you seen a man dressed in a locksmith uniform." He repeated the description of the man Felicity had spoke with.

Lachlan frowned. "He sounds familiar, but if it's the same person, he was dressed in street clothes when he was in here. He met with a quiet, cute girl. Brunette with big blue eyes. She mentioned she had just moved into the neighborhood. A couple of weeks ago if I remember right."

Bile and stomach acid roiled in Johanna's gut. The girl Lachlan described could be Monica.

"You two going to tell me what's really going on here?" Lachlan's eyebrow rose to emphasize his question.

"Mrs. Cresswell was attacked in her flat this evening," Johanna said.

Lachlan straightened and his expression grew dark and ugly. "And you think this guy did that?"

"He's a suspect," Rick said.

"You a bobbie?" Lachlan gave Rick a suspicious look.

"No, he's a private consultant I hired," Johanna said softly. She glanced around the bar. They were definitely attracting attention. Attention that could possibly tip off her harasser. "We think it's related to some bizarre love letters I started receiving last month. Mrs. Cresswell may have suspected the man—"

"Doesn't she use Johnny Westcott's service?" Lachlan interjected. "Nearly everyone around here does."

"She called someone else," Johanna replied.

"Because you thought Johnny was behind the letter?" Lachlan's left eyebrow rose to the same level as the right.

"Because someone with keys entered Doctor Ridgeley's flat and vandalized it," Rick stated firmly.

"Well, she never trusted me with a key, so you can cross me off your list, Sherlock," Lachlan snapped.

"He's not accusing you—" Johanna started.

"Yes, he is," Lachlan snapped at the same time Rick said, "Yes, I am."

"Is every ex of Doctor Jo's on your little list?" Lachlan glared at Rick.

"With your temper, it appears I do need to add you." Rick's face was calm, but tension spilled from him as fast as the blood from Mrs. Cresswell's head wound.

"Stop," Johanna snapped. "Both of you. Now."

Rick and Lachlan turned to look at her.

"I'm only going to say this once." She eyed both men. "Richard, Lachlan and I had an amicable split. It was never serious between us."

"Well, that depends on how you define serious—" Lachlan began. Johanna raised her right index finger, and he stopped.

"Lachlan, Richard was recommended to me by another ex so untwist your knickers," she said. "He's doing his job, but by him guarding me, whoever is sending me those letters assaulted an elderly woman I care about to make a point."

"I apologize, Doctor Ridgeley," Rick said.

"Sorry, Doctor Jo." Lachlan shot an appraising glance at Rick. "But are you sure he's not helping his buddy?"

Johanna looked at Rick. "You do realize he has a valid point, don't you?"

"Yes, and you're a very smart woman, so I'm surprised you haven't accused me of it before now," Rick said evenly.

Johanna took a huge gulp of her pint. This whole situation was getting ridiculously complicated. Everything in her life seemed to be blowing up around her. Even though she'd sworn off Club Noir while she was an SHO, maybe she should stop by tonight. There was always a sub in the wings looking for a master to play with. Inflicting some pain would take the edge off her anxiety over Mrs. Cresswell's injuries.

"Finish your beer, Richard." She gave him a pointed look. "I need to make one more stop tonight."

Chapter Fifteen

Rick downed his beer. Between the lager at dinner and the Irish red now, he wasn't drunk, but he also prayed Johanna wasn't intoxicated enough to want to do something stupid.

Or dangerous.

Johanna gulped the last of her mug and set down the glassware. "A pleasure to see you again, Lachlan." She pivoted on her heel and stalked out of the pub.

Rick moved to follow her, but Lachlan called out, "Hey, man, wait."

Rick hesitated before he looked over his shoulder.

"Watch out for her," Lachlan muttered. "And don't make the same mistake I did."

"What mistake is that?" Rick found himself genuinely interested.

"Being a doctor is the most important thing in her life." Lachlan actually looked despondent. "Don't push her to be something else."

Rick slowly nodded. That had been his own assessment as well from the moment he met her. "I'll keep that in mind."

"And I haven't been back to her house since we called it quits." Lachlan's mouth twisted into a rueful grin. "No matter how many times Felicity has asked."

"Understood." Rick nodded and headed for the door. Despite what Johanna thought, it wasn't just men who had a problem understanding the word "no".

Thankfully, Johanna waited for him on the pavement. "Should I ask?"

"Lachlan . . ." Rick wasn't sure how much to say.

She folded her arms over her chest. "Lachlan what?"

"You broke his heart, but I don't think he's a suspect."

"Broke his heart?" Her arms dropped to her sides. "We both agreed it was a casual thing. Until he got—" An appalled expression appeared. "That's why he was pushing so hard during med school finals." Her shoulders sagged. "Why didn't I see what was happening?"

"Because you're a very focused woman." Rick placed his hand on the small of her back and guided her in the direction of Mrs. Cresswell's antique automobile. "Where did you need to go next?"

"Club Noir," she said briskly.

He halted in mid-step and faced her. "Why?"

"You can do some more investigating," she said, but she refused to look at him.

"While you?" he prompted.

She closed her eyes. "I need to take care of some personal needs."

"Oh." He wiped his hand over his face. Various parts of him warred inside on how to handle this. The security expert said it was a damn stupid idea. The jealous part didn't want Johanna around a potential rival. The submissive, the part he hid so carefully for all these years, wanted to beg her to use him if it kept her safe.

"Aren't you going to argue with me about it?" The streetlight overhead put her arch expression in stark relief.

"Right now, I'm too busy arguing with myself," he muttered.

"What are you saying?" she murmured. "Are you . . . volunteering?"

Rick's heart stopped. She was giving him the opportunity to state what he wanted. "If it means preventing this bastard from harming you, then yes. I'll do whatever you need me to do."

"And you'll obey my every command without question?" She placed her palm over his heart. No doubt she could feel it pounding.

"As long as we have a safeword I can use to indicate there is an issue with your security." When he saw the hesitation in her eyes, he leaned close and whispered, "Please, Mistress. For Faddil's sake if not mine. Neither of us want anything to happen to you."

Johanna slowly nodded. "Very well. Your offer is accepted."

Rick followed Johanna's directions. They pulled into what appeared to be an alley, but in fact was a private drive. Few windows faced the obscured entrance. He suspected the club owned the building across the street.

The drive wove around a garden that appeared to be full of spring color beneath the old Bentley's headlights. As he braked in front of a grand entrance, a doorman scrambled down the steps to open the passenger door.

"Mistress Johanna, a pleasure to see you again."

She inclined her head as if she were the Princess of Wales herself. "And you, Walter."

A valet approached Rick and handed him a ticket.

"Not a scratch on the mistress's vehicle," Rick said under his breath.

"Never," the valet whispered. The boy didn't even meet Rick's eyes.

Rick circled the front of the car and stood a pace behind and to the right of Johanna, keeping his head down but watching for problems by his peripheral vision. It had been a long time since he submitted to anyone, but he'd forgotten to ask Johanna, and it had been the proscribed position of his old Domme. He trusted Johanna to correct him if she preferred something else.

He followed her up the steps and into the foyer. The building was middle-aged by London standards. Late fifteenth or early sixteenth century if he had to guess from the style of the wainscoting and panels. Whoever was responsible kept the interior in immaculate condition. His leather soles sank into the plush burgundy carpet.

Johanna's entire manner changed when they entered the building. She was self-confident before. Now . . . hell, she'd have the Queen Mum groveling at her feet.

They approached a podium where a balding man in a proper butler's uniform bowed. "Mistress Johanna, a pleasure to see you again. It's been far too long." He eyed Rick like he was the dead rat in Johanna's refrigerator. "A guest?"

"This is Richard Paine, my new pet."

One of the butler's bushy white eyebrow tried to replace the hair on his head. "You know the rules, Mistress Johanna. I need to record all legal names of guests."

"Please show Colby your identification, Richard," she murmured, but the sly smile she gave him was pure sin.

Rick could understand the butler's suspicion, especially in a place like this. He pulled out his wallet, slid his driving license from the slot, and handed it to Colby. The butler pursed his lips when he realized Johanna was telling the truth about Rick's surname. Colby wrote the information into the huge black book with cream-colored pages that sat on the podium before he handed the license back to Rick.

"The usual room, Mistress," he asked.

"If it's available, yes, please," she said.

Colby rang the little silver bell on top of his podium. A woman emerged from a door behind the butler. Similar to him, she wore a proper maid's uniform. She stopped in front of Johanna and curtsied. When the girl straightened, Colby whispered instructions in her ear.

The maid smiled. "This way, Mistress."

They followed her through a confusing maze of hallways and up two flights of stairs. The maid stopped before a black-lacquered door and curtsied again.

"The Queen of Scots room as you requested, Mistress." The girl straightened. "Is there anything else you require?" The way she eyed Rick made him wonder what other services the staff offered.

"No, thank you. That will be all," Johanna replied.

The girl tried to hide her disappointment as she trotted down the hallway toward the last staircase they had climbed. Rick took a deep breath to quell his nerves and stood at parade rest.

"Are you trying to imply you are ready, Richard?" Johanna drawled.

"What would you like my proscribed position to be, Mistress?" He focused on the white rose on the wallpaper behind her left elbow.

"You've been trained before?" She sounded suspicious, but he didn't dare look her in the eye.

"Yes, Mistress."

"Does the minister or the emir know?"

"The minister is aware, but that's not the reason he recommended me for this assignment." Was this why he missed the army? Because he enjoyed being told what to do?

"Then why did he recommend you to Faddil?" she demanded.

"Because he knows I can be discreet."

"And what have you been discreet about for the minister?"

This time, he looked her directly in the eyes. Whatever punishment she inflicted would be worth proving himself to her.

"If I told you, then I would lose my reputation for discretion, Mistress."

Humor flared in her eyes, and she struggled to keep her face straight. When she regained her composure. "Since I haven't told you my rules, I'll let this instance slide." She twisted the knob and pushed the door open. He followed her inside, praying he'd made the right decision.

Chapter Sixteen

Johanna watched Rick examine the room while she locked the door and turned on the red light in the hallway indicating "Do Not Disturb".

The Queen of Scots room was how she remembered it. The club administrator hadn't changed a thing. The black lights brought out the neon figures on the wall. Paintings of men and women in various positions of erotic torture. Soft black tumbling mats covered the floor.

The rack and the Saint Andrews cross stood in the far corners. The only other door in the room was to her left. The door stood open and revealed a sink. Further inside the bathroom was a toilet and a shower. To her right was a fold-out couch for the submissive's recovery. Between the main entrance and the bathroom was a counter and cabinets full of brand new supplies and toys. Membership dues paid for everything in order to keep participants as safe as possible. AIDS and HIV were serious issues, which was why certain activities were no longer permitted within the club.

Rick showed no particular interest or dislike of the equipment in the room. No, he would be the type where the real test was self-control. Being physically restrained wouldn't have the same challenge to him.

"Richard," she said softly.

He turned toward her, his gaze downcast. "Yes, Mistress?"

"'Blueberry' is our word to begin a scene," she said. "'Pomegranate' is our word to stop."

"Yes, Mistress."

"Normally, I go over all my rules before a sub even steps inside my dungeon." She circled around him, but he didn't move a muscle. "However, these are unusual circumstances."

"Yes, Mistress."

His obedience sent a wave of relief through her. She was in control, if only of this experience. The tension in her back and shoulders since the break-in yesterday eased.

Johanna approached him and trailed her fingertips up the left arm of Rick's jacket. "We don't know each other very well. Trust is already difficult to build between two people under normal conditions." She continued tracing a path across his broad shoulders. "However, you've made more of an effort to build my trust over the last thirty hours than anyone has ever done in thirty months. I respect that." Her fingers traveled down the right sleeve, enjoying the hard muscle beneath the fine wool. "But I will not tolerate you letting you push yourself too far in a misguided effort to please me. Is that understood, Richard?"

"Yes, Mistress." The muscle of his jaw clenched in his effort to stay still, but the tenting of his trousers left no question as to his feelings.

Or his desire.

"Do you have any questions before we begin?"

His Adam's apple bobbed. "Yes, Mistress."

Good. He wasn't going into this scene without knowledge, like some idiots she'd encountered. "You may ask," she whispered.

This time, he looked directly in her eyes. "Why did you start calling me Rick this afternoon?"

Out of all the possible questions she expected, this was not one. She inhaled deeply. "Because it is your preferred version of your name, and you earned the right to be called by it in public."

Something flickered deep in his eyes. An emotion and another question, but his face smoothed as if he answered his own curiosity. And it made her wonder what he had been about to ask her.

"What else did you want to say?" She cupped his cheek. Stubble met her palm. She generally preferred her subs clean-shaven, but for some reason, the facial hair sent a thrill through her.

"Nothing, Mistress."

She smiled. "Richard, what were you about to ask me?"

His warm breath tickled her arm. "Why you switched back to using my full given name when we arrived at the club. But I understand it is your choice to call me whatever you wish during a session. Forgive me for not comprehending right away, Mistress."

"We've both experienced a great deal more stress than normal over the last two days." She ran her fingers through his hair. "Such a lapse before we start is forgivable. However—" She eased closer until their lips were only millimeters apart. "Remember you don't have to think during this session. Only experience."

Anticipation lay in his gaze. He licked his lips before he said, "Yes, Mistress."

"Do you have any other questions?"

He swallowed before he said, "No, Mistress."

"Very well then." She stepped back. "Blueberry."

His attention dropped to the floor. She definitely needed to ask him about his previous Domme. But later. For now, they both required a little of their own type of stress relief.

"Take off your clothing." She pointed at the full-sized cupboard. "Hang your suit, shirt and tie in there. Shoes go in the bottom. Everything else needs to be folded and laid on the top shelf. When you are finished, kneel on the center mat to indicate you are ready to begin."

Johanna propped her right hip on the couch arm and watched Richard disrobe. His motions were quick. Efficient.

Even though she guessed him to be a decade or so older than her, his body was lean. Hard. Which meant he kept up his exercise routine after being discharged from the service. He wasn't self-conscious about his erection either. When he turned to hang up his clothing, she had a view of his delectable ass.

Along with the multitude of scars that traced from his waist down to his calves. Shrapnel scars. As much as she wanted to ask about them, now was not the time.

He crossed to the center mat and knelt with his hands behind his back. Since this was their first time, she need a simple, elegant tool. She stalked over to the cupboards and opened the top one closest to the main door. A single tail whip hung there.

Johanna glanced over her shoulder. Richard still knelt on the center mat, his gaze firmly fix on a spot on the floor in front of him. Whoever his first Domme had been, she'd done an excellent job. And the previous Domme had been a fool to let him escape.

Her pussy clenched with her own need. She pulled open the drawer below and selected a purple condom. Her favorite color. It glowed neon through the clear plastic wrap thanks to the black lights in the room.

A pity she didn't have any of her outfits with her. After the insanity of the day, she hadn't even had a chance to change out of her skirt, blouse, or sensible shoes from the hospital.

She set the whip on the counter, kicked off her shoes, and removed her tights and panties before she tucked the condom package inside her cleavage, a reminder not to overwork Richard. Not if she wanted him to satisfy all her needs tonight.

Johanna picked up the single tail once again and slipped her right hand through the wrist strap. She tightened her grip on the handle and flicked her wrist. Richard jerked at the first practice snap of her whip, though she aimed at the floor mat behind him. After two years, the last thing she wanted was to accidentally cause real harm because she had been so lax on her own training.

The next two snaps didn't produce the slightest muscle twitch from him. How long had it been since he had a session? Was that the real reason he wanted to be here with her? To get the release he craved, not because he was truly attracted to her?

She squelched that train of thought. His motives didn't matter. She wanted to be here to relieve her own anxieties, and she hadn't planned on his participation. Any submissive would have done.

Wouldn't they?

Johanna cleared her mind. Cluttered thoughts led to accidents and real injuries. She shifted her hips and flicked her wrist. The popper landed on his right shoulder with a sharp crack, right where she intended.

Maybe this was like riding the proverbial bicycle.

She delivered five more strikes in quick succession over various places on his back and shoulders. Never the same place twice. Only on the last hit did Richard grunt. Maybe he taken her lecture to heart about denying his discomfort after all.

The wicked part of her wanted to lash him until he cried out in pain. That was part of the delight in working over heterosexual males. Getting them to release the emotions Western society forced them to keep in check. Johanna stalked back and forth on the pad behind Richard, calculating the responses she wanted.

A seventh strike. This one to Richard's left buttock. This time, he moaned softly.

The eighth strike went to a space above one of the scars on the side of his right thigh. The ninth licked his right buttock. Still, he didn't so much as flinch.

Ten more cracks of the whip, over his back, shoulders, and ass. Her arm muscles started to ache. It was her own fault for not practicing in her flat, or coming here, rather than falling on her couch and watching the telly after every shift at the hospital.

However, her rapid breathing had nothing to do with her exertion, any more than Richard's pants did.

"Lay down on your back." Johanna toss the whip aside as he obeyed. Once he was prone, she knelt beside him. Curiosity of what she would do next shone in his gaze. She grabbed the condom from her cleavage, tore open the clear plastic, and rolled it down the length of his cock. His erection twitched when she pushed up her skirt and swung her right knee over to straddle him.

"You did very well for our first time." She smiled at him while she guided his erection inside of her. Damn, it felt so good, so right, sliding down his cock. Why, oh why, did she think she could get through the last of her studies without a man inside of her? And Richard filled her completely.

His eyes were closed and his hands curled into fists against the mat as she rode his body. She took a little sympathy on him.

Johanna leaned forward and placed her palms on each side of his head. "You may look at me and touch me, Richard."

His eyelids flashed open. His hands reached underneath her hiked skirt and palmed her ass, squeezing and molding her flesh as they moved together. His lips parted.

She responded to his unspoken request and straightened. Her hips shifted while she slowly unbuttoned her blouse. The desire in his eyes flamed her own to new heights.

Johanna tossed her blouse aside. Her bra followed. Richard reached for her breasts. He traced delicate circles around her areolas.

"No." The sound was more a moan from her throat than a word. She couldn't deal with his gentleness, not after what happened to Mrs. Cresswell. "Pinch them," she ordered.

The sharp pain of his nails in her flesh shot a mix of pleasure and agony to her core. Her internal muscles clenched, squeezing his cock.

His hands went back to her ass cheeks. He drove deeper into her while she ground her mound against him. Their motions became a frenzied dance, an ode to the violence that forced the universe into existence.

Richard stiffened beneath her thighs. His cock pulsed inside of her. Johanna couldn't breathe as every muscle seized and blackness obscured her vision. She fell head first in the whirlpool of ecstasy and pain.

Chapter Seventeen

Johanna collapsed across Rick's chest and tried to catch her breath. Sex and all of its components had never been something she shied away from, but she hadn't had an orgasm that intense since she discovered masturbation.

"Pomegranate," she murmured between pants.

Rick reached for her hair and released the clip that kept it out of her way while she was on duty. He stroked the escaped locks from her perspiring face and neck.

"What are you doing?" she said.

"I've been imagining your hair down and brushing it for you since the first moment I saw you." He gulped air, and his heart still pounded beneath her cheek. "I apologize if I've overstepped."

His cock slipped from her, and she rolled off him and onto the mat. She took a shuddering breath. What made her have sex with him? They barely knew each other. Was it the stress of the recent harassment? Or had she made a mistake forgoing any relationship for the last two years?

"Did I displease you in some way?" Rick rolled on his side and propped his head on his fist as he regarded her.

"No, I—" She licked her suddenly dry lips before she could look at him. "I should have grabbed a change of clothes and brought them with me, so we could stay the night."

"They have like . . . hotel rooms here?"

She laughed at the absurd expression on his face. "Not everyone wants a 24/7 BDSM relationship. So yes, the club has conventional rooms for members and guests' downtime."

"No offense, but this place must cost a fortune." He gestured with his free hand.

"Yes, it does, but members pay a percentage based on their gross income."

"So you pay a little less than, say, the emir?"

"Now, I do." She hesitated. If she told him how the club's system worked, he might chose to find another Domme. For some reason, her heart couldn't bear the thought. "I had a sponsor in the beginning."

"We could stay here for the night if you'd like," he said haltingly. "Get up early, and hit our flats for a change of clothing. I'm assuming the club provides soap and toothpaste."

They could get separate rooms, but from his expression, he needed more. Could she actually sleep with a sub? The closest she'd ever come was staying in the bed until her sub fell asleep after a play session.

"They do." Johanna stared at the ceiling. She'd screwed up by not interviewing Rick thoroughly before entering a play room with him. Big time. She needed to fix this. She rolled onto her side to face him and mirrored his position.

"Before we go any farther, you need to tell me about your previous Domme," she said.

His expression hardened. "There's nothing to tell."

"That very response means there is, and I've apparently hit a trigger with you," she added softly.

He rolled onto his back, but she didn't miss his wince. Had she gone too far with his whipping? "I'd prefer not to talk about this right now."

"Then it's best we go back to my flat." Johanna hated to manipulate him in this manner, but it was a necessary ploy to get him to open up. She pushed herself into a sitting position and started searching for her discarded clothing.

"I know you're trying to care for me in your own way, but can we discuss this in one of the hotel rooms? In the dark?" His tone was straightforward, but his expression pleaded with her to grant him this one small mercy.

"Very well." She scowled at him. "But if you don't answer my questions, this will be our last time together. I will throw you and that damn dead rat you left in my refrigerator out onto the street. Is that understood?"

"Yes, Mistress."

"Put your shirt, trousers, and shoes back on while I make arrangements," she ordered.

"Yes, Mistress." But there was no cockiness in his voice or manner at getting her to spend the night with him. Only relief that she wasn't leaving him alone.

Colby must have anticipated her change in plans. Johanna no sooner voiced her request when he handed her a key and said, "Have a pleasant evening, Mistress Johanna."

She retrieved Rick and led him to the fourth floor suite. A huge king-sized bed dominated the room. The walls and bedspread were a soft lavender color. The décor was simple and understated for the type of building that housed the club. She smiled that Colby remembered her preferences.

"The facilities are in there." She gestured at the doorway in the far right corner of the room. "Clean up, and then I'll take care of your back."

"Take care of my back?" Rick cocked his head.

"Rub on ointment," she said.

"May I please ask that you don't?"

She frowned. "Why not?"

"I—" The corners of his mouth twitched. "I would like to enjoy the pain if you don't mind."

Johanna considered his request before she said, "All right, but if I noticed the pain interrupting your sleep, I will put the ointment on your back."

"Yes, Mistress." He inclined his head before he turned and entered the lavatory. Behind the closed door, the rush of water running signaled he was doing as she asked.

Whatever was she going to do about Rick? She had broken her own vow not to use him in less than two days. And she had a feeling that even once her harasser was caught, it would be very difficult to get Rick Paine out of her life.

Or her heart.

Chapter Eighteen

Once the lights were off in their room and Johanna and Rick were entwined beneath the covers, she murmured, "Tell me about her."

Deep down, he knew Johanna wouldn't let go of the subject of Annette. But a little part of him had hoped Johanna would fall asleep tonight before she did ask. Not to mention it was uncomfortable talking about Annette while naked and in bed with another woman. But he might as well·deal with the subject. Johanna would press, just as Annette would have if the women's positions were reversed.

"I met her when I was a soldier." Damn, his heart still ached after all these years. "I was twenty-three, just beginning to figure out what I was. I joined the army because I wanted someone to tell me what to do. I just didn't understand my real need was for my bed partner to do so, not anyone else, until I had signed the papers." He couldn't help chuckling at his naiveté all those years ago.

"She understood my career was important to me, and she often met me on my leaves wherever I was stationed." The old pain rose in his throat. "But when I got back from the Falklands, she refused to see me." His chest ached.

"Did she say why?" Johanna stroked his hair, trying to offer comfort.

"No." He swallowed hard to dislodge the lump. "She merely said it was over between us. That I needed to find another Domme. And to stop calling her or visiting."

"I'm sorry," she whispered. "That was a cruel thing to do to you."

"The worst part is she died alone in a hospice six months later." He blinked to ease the burning in his eyes. "I would have been there for her. No one should have to die alone."

"No, they shouldn't." They were both quiet for a long time before Johanna added, "That was unnecessary pain, and I'm sorry you had to endure such a thing."

Her voice had a hint of anger, and he could guess what caused it. It was the same reason she needed the session in the club's play room.

"What happened to Mrs. Cresswell was not your fault, Johanna."

She sighed. "Intellectually I know that. It's just . . ."

"Just what?" he murmured.

"I dislike not being in total control of a situation." There was a hint of bitterness in her words.

For some reason, he didn't think she was referring to her stalker. "Who was it you couldn't save?"

She sighed again. "It doesn't matter."

He turned on his side and propped himself on his elbow. "It matters if you're flogging yourself over it after all these years."

"You're one to talk." She tried to tease, but her tone had an edge to it.

"I refuse to repeat my past mistakes," he said. "I should have pressed with Annette. You may be the Domme in our relationship, but that doesn't mean I won't take care of you. Serve you properly. Even if that means pressing an uncomfortable subject."

"A relationship?"

Rick cursed at himself silently. He couldn't see Johanna's face in the dark room, but he had the distinct impression she scowled at him.

"Would you prefer a different term, Mistress?"

"We barely know each other," she murmured. "You're jumping to conclusions over a session we both needed to take the edge off our emotions."

"Very well, Mistress," he answered through clenched teeth. Damn, he knew how to pick unemotionally unavailable Dommes. He rolled onto his sore back. Maybe the pain would remind him to keep his feelings to himself.

"Richard."

His body responded to her voice and private name for him despite his anger. "Yes, Mistress."

"It was my mother. She had a heart attack in our kitchen while she was making dinner. I sat at the kitchen table, doing my school work." Johanna's voice cracked in her recitation. "Even though I'd learned CPR and I tried . . . she died on the floor. Everyone kept telling me there was nothing I could have done . . ."

Her body shuddered with silent sobs. Rick scooted closer and pulled her into his arms. He stroked her hair while she released her grief.

Losing her mother that way explained a lot about Johanna. But how the hell did he convince her that he would never leave?

Chapter Nineteen

When the alarm clock went off the next morning, Johanna and Rick dressed without a word. She didn't know what to say to him after her emotional breakdown last night in bed. Only her medical training kept her head on straight when she saw Mrs. Cresswell lying on her living room floor.

Neither Johanna nor her father dealt well with Mum's sudden passing. He had moved to Scotland once she was out of primary school. The last card she received from him was mailed in Australia. They never talked about Mum again after the funeral.

When Lachlan started talking about marriage, she shoved him out her door, claiming she needed to focus on her last three years of practical programmes. So much for dealing with her internal anguish in a healthy matter.

Rick called down for their car. Johanna didn't recognize the morning butler, though he addressed her by name. She had to bite her lip to keep from snapping at the man when he said he looked forward to seeing her again.

The drive back to her flat was equally silent, but strangely, it was a comfortable silence. Rick didn't press her to talk about last night. He didn't seem to hold her breakdown against her either. He parked in the tiny garage at the back of the property, but he didn't move to get out.

"Can you call in sick today?" he asked.

"Not if I want to check in on Mrs. Cresswell." Johanna regarded him. "Why should I call off my shift?"

"Because whoever's behind this has access to the hospital as well as your building." He eyed her. "And I want to change the damn locks on the building myself. I can't watch you at the hospital if I'm doing that."

"Can we compromise on this matter?" she offered.

"That depends on what you mean." Suspicion glinted from his eyes.

"Take me to Tower Hospital. Escort me to the women's locker room if you must." She gestured emphatically. "But my harasser isn't going to try anything while I'm on rounds. There are simply too many witnesses.

"You have Felicity's number, and you can drop off her new keys at her office. I'll warn Monica of the locks being changed again. When you return to the hospital, we'll make sure she and Mrs. Cresswell get copies of the new keys."

She waited while he mused over her ideas.

"All right," he finally murmured. "That's acceptable. However—" He gestured at the house. "I am going inside first to check things." He held out his palm.

She placed her keys into his waiting hand without argument. Her predator had gone from annoying to dangerous. She'd be a fool not to heed Rick's advice, regardless of what happened between them last night.

Nothing looked out of ordinary as they exited the garage and crossed the back garden. The rear door of the Georgian was even still locked. White powder drifted down when Rick unlocked the door.

"What on earth—"

He grinned at her over his shoulder. "Don't worry. I placed it there."

"Using your fingerprint powder as an indicator if someone entered after we left last night?"

He nodded and stepped into the hallway. She followed and closed the door, flipping the deadbolt as she went.

Rick checked the doors to Mrs. Cresswell and Monica's flats. Both entrances were still locked tight. His shoulders tightened as he examined the front door to the building, but he didn't touch it.

"What's wrong?" she murmured.

"Powder on the doorknob." He examined the doorjamb before he crouched and looked at the knob again. "Someone rattled the front door hard enough to disturb the powder, but most of this should have fallen onto the floor when they twisted the knob to enter."

Johanna frowned. "We already gave keys to the other girls."

"And we suspect Mrs. Cresswell's assailant probably has duplicates off all the keys to the building and flats." Rick shook his head. "There's nowhere to hide in the hallway." He straightened and headed for the staircase.

Johanna's heart pounded as she followed him up the steps. At the landing, he checked Felicity's door to ensure it was still locked before he turned to Johanna's flat.

He inserted and twisted the key, then pushed the door open. She breathed a sigh of relief when the powder drifted down from the top of the door.

She followed Rick into her flat. Nothing appeared to have been touched since they left last night to take Felicity to the Tube station. In fact, her kitchen still had the oily smell of the fish and chips wrappers laying in her rubbish bin.

Johanna and Rick looked at each other.

"Do you have a change of clothes?" she asked.

He shook his head. "I planned on swinging by my flat and packing a bag after I escort you to the hospital. If you don't mind me using your phone, I'd like to call the emir, and let him know the status of your case."

"Please tell him, I'll pay you for your time," she insisted. Faddil had done so much for her. She couldn't bear the thought of him spending another pound for her security.

Especially after she'd had her way with said personal security consultant.

"No," Rick stated.

"But I'm the one—" she started.

"With all due respect, Mistress, I am not a gigolo," he snapped. "My contract is with the emir. Not you."

Johanna took a deep breath to keep from snapping back. She'd had the same argument with Faddil at the beginning of their relationship. "I can see where you would think that. But your time and expertise are valuable. And I would still pay Faddil back for your fee. I'm merely cutting out multiple exchanges of the same money."

"And he warned me you'd do just that." Rick's expression relaxed. "I don't want to fight with you, but the emir made his wishes quite clear in the matter. His recommendation would go a long way to building my fledgling company's reputation." His lips twitched. "Unless you're truly in the market for a male escort."

She knew he was trying to get a rise from her, but she threw her hands into the air anyway. "Do as you wish. I need to get ready for work." She pivoted and marched into her bedroom. She'd whip that pleased-with-himself expression off Rick's face the first chance she got.

One of the hospital security guards waited for her when she walked through the main entrance of Tower Hospital. "Doctor Ridgeley, the administrator wishes to speak with you."

"Why?" A chill ran through her. "What's happening?"

"That's between you and him, Doctor."

When Rick moved to follow her, the security guard held up his hand. "I'm sorry, sir. This is private hospital business."

Rick produced his identification. "Doctor Ridgeley's life has been threatened and her flat broken into. I've been hired as her bodyguard. Given some of the insults and harassment that have been dished out by people within the hospital, and therefore, making them suspects, I am not leaving her side."

The guard worked his jaw a few times before he decided the argument was above his paygrade. "Fine." He pivoted on his heel and charged toward the elevator bank. Johanna had to jog to keep up. It was a good thing she'd bought the orthopedic shoes for work.

The lift remained quiet as it climbed to the top floor. All the nerves Johanna thought she'd worked off during last night's play session with Rick assailed her. What could the hospital administrator want with her?

Had Roger Bennett complained about whatever Rick had said to him privately yesterday? She cast a surreptitious glance at her sub. He seemed as confused about the summons as she felt, though she doubted most people would pick up on the subtle cues in his body language.

The lift doors slid open, and the three of them walked into the administrator's office. His secretary looked at the entrants with a stern expression on her face. Her mouth formed a moue of distaste. "He's waiting for you, Doctor Ridgeley."

As if she were a half-hour late for her shift instead of being a half-hour early like she always was.

"Thank you," Johanna murmured. She crossed to the inner office, Rick at her side.

"Sir, you can't go in there!" the secretary screeched.

Both Johanna and Rick ignored her. She pushed the door open. Inside were her supervisor Doctor Bennett, the head of security Mister Cunningham, and the hospital administrator himself. "You wished to see me, Doctor Darlington?"

"Just you, Doctor Ridgeley." He didn't really snap at her, but his tone brooked no argument.

However, as she had come to expect, Rick argued anyway.

He stepped forward. "As I've explained to the other people in this room and the security guard you sent to fetch Doctor Ridgeley, her life has been threatened and her flat broken into. Additionally, Doctor

Ridgeley's landlady was attacked yesterday afternoon, quite possibly by the same person who has been harassing the good doctor. Given the circumstances, I will be present for this meeting."

A little thrill went through Johanna. This was a different side of Rick, the army officer side. The side that got the mission done no matter the odds. She found herself liking it.

"Close the door if you insist on staying." This time, Doctor Darlington did snap.

However, Rick did as he ordered.

"Doctor Ridgeley, now that I've heard your bodyguard's side, as well as Doctor Bennett and Mist Cunningham's, what the devil is your side to this matter?"

Johanna laid out the recent events calmly and clearly, as if she'd been called upon to recite the symptoms, diagnosis and treatment of a patient. Except she left out Faddil's part. Instead, she said Minister Wynton-Smythe had recommended Rick as a security consultant.

When she finished, Doctor Darlington leaned back in his chair and contemplated her. "You should have contacted Mister Cunningham when this started."

"The original letters were all sent to my home address, sir," Johanna replied. "It wasn't hospital business."

"But the rat in your locker is," he pointed out. "And you should have called the police."

"Sir, her stalker didn't escalate his actions until I became involved," Rick interjected. "He probably feels I'm a threat to him—"

"I don't need a lecture in psychological hogwash by someone with less experience than Mister Cunningham!" Doctor Darlington snapped. "Doctor Ridgeley, I'm placing you on leave until you can get your personal affairs in order. I do not want this kind of chaos in my hospital!"

Blood roared her ears. This forced leave was ridiculous. Blaming her for the stalker's actions was unfair. Was Darlington simply looking for a reason to get rid of her?

"Sir, with all due respect, there is no reason for putting me on leave," Johanna said. "This has nothing to do with my medical skill or my integrity as a physician."

"It has everything to do with unreported biohazardous waste in the women's locker room." Darlington replied. "Not to mention its improper disposal. It puts the health and safety of my staff at risk, and that, I will not tolerate."

"Doctor Darlington—" She tried again, but he was having none of it.

"All of you, get out," Darlington yelled. "Some of us have real work to do."

Doctor Bennett and Mister Cunningham rose and followed Johanna and Rick out of both Doctor Darlington and his secretary's offices.

Once they were well out of earshot, Johanna whirled around and poked a finger in Bennett's chest. "This is your doing, isn't it?"

"No, it isn't," Mister Cunningham said. "And it wasn't mine either. Darlington knew about the rat in your locker before he called us up to his office."

Bennett shook his head. "I swear, Johanna. I didn't say a damn thing to anybody about our talk yesterday morning." He glanced at Mister Cunningham. "And I didn't know about the dead rat until Bob told me in the lift on our way up here. I even tried to talk Darlington out of the leave of absence."

"He did, too." Mister Cunningham nodded. "But the old man had his mind made up before you even got here."

Johanna wanted to drop to the floor. What the hell was she supposed to do now? But this wasn't only about her. She steeled herself for another fight.

"Before you toss me out on my bum, can I check on Mrs. Cresswell? She's my landlady who was admitted last night."

Bennett and Cunningham surprised her by both of them nodding.

Rick added, "Can Doctor Ridgeley stay long enough for me to run an errand? I don't want to leave her alone at her flat."

Cunningham grinned. "The administrator didn't say she couldn't visit a friend. She just can't be practicing medicine while she's here."

Even Bennett smirked at the security chief's assessment. "That is true."

Relief flooded Johanna. If nothing else went right today, she could at least keep her promise to her flatmates and check on their landlady.

She just prayed Mrs. Cresswell would recover. She couldn't bear it if her landlady didn't.

Chapter Twenty

The last thing Rick wanted to do was leave Johanna alone at the hospital, but Mister Cunningham promised to check on her every ten minutes while Rick drove to his flat and the hardware shop.

"I didn't appreciate the dressing down the administrator gave me over that dead rat being placed in Doctor Ridgeley's locker," Cunningham grumbled. "I've got a vested interest in helping you catch this wanker. And I doubt he'll suspect the doctor will be in another ward."

Johanna located Mrs. Cresswell's floor and room. When they arrived and entered, a blond young man sat beside Mrs. Cresswell's bed and held her terribly pale hand. Mrs. Cresswell herself was sound asleep.

"Isaac?" Johanna murmured.

"Doctor Ridgeley," Isaac said stiffly as he stood. "May I speak with you outside?"

This must be the nephew. Rick quickly sized him up. Isaac was, a good ten centimeters shorter than Rick, and just under twelve stone. He barely looked a day over twenty. Hardly a threat under normal circumstances, but obsession could drive a man to do strange things. While he may not have been the person to assault his aunt, it didn't mean he hadn't hired someone or bribed the real locksmith.

"Of course," she murmured.

Cunningham shot Rick a questioning look. Rick in turn tilted his flat hand side to side to indicate Isaac might be a suspect. A grim look settled on the security chief's face as they followed Johanna and Isaac out of Mrs. Cresswell's room.

"What happened yesterday?" Isaac hissed once the door to his aunt's room swung shut. "The police told me someone who's been following you was behind the attack."

A jolt rant through Rick at the lack of intelligence, much less propriety by the bobbies who'd contacted Isaac. Those idiots could have blown the case if Isaac was behind this.

"Can you start from the beginning, Isaac?" Rick said.

"Who the bloody hell are you?" the younger man snapped.

"Richard Paine is my bodyguard," Johanna said sternly. "He and I are concerned about your aunt. We're the ones who found her. And yes, we think the person who has been harassing me is the one who hurt her."

All the anger seemed to rush out of Isaac. He slumped against the hallway wall. "I can't believe someone would have hurt Aunt Lavender. She's the strongest person I know."

Rick pulled out his notebook and pen from his jacket pocket. "When was the last time you were at your aunt's house?"

"Yesterday." He looked up at Rick. "I take it you're the one who changed the locks. I went over to the house to pick up some things for her, and my key didn't work."

"No, it wasn't me," Rick said. "But we have to assume the stalker has copies of the new keys because one of the tenants met him coming out after the ambulance left and we escorted the third tenant to the bus stop so she could stay at a friend's place for the night. Where were you yesterday afternoon before the police contacted you?"

The younger man's shoulders and neck tensed. "You think I had something to do with any of this?"

"It's my job to check out everyone." Rick shrugged. "It's nothing personal. Our only leads indicate a man is behind this, and he has keys to the building."

Isaac frowned and shook his head. "The only people who have keys that I know of is me, Aunt Lavender, and the tenants. Have you checked with Aunt Lavender's regular locksmith?"

"She was concerned she couldn't trust them, so she planned to call someone else to change the locks after someone broke into my flat the day before yesterday," Johanna interjected.

"You still haven't answered Mister Paine about where you were yesterday?" Cunningham prompted.

"I was working." Isaac said. "I drive a lorry for a beer distributor. Both the store managers and I have to sign on deliveries. You can contact my employer to verify where I was and that it was me driving."

Rick scribbled down the name of Isaac's manager and his contact details. "Did you have today off? It's only Thursday."

"I took a personal day after the bobbies called me last night." Isaac wrapped his arms about himself. "My parents are on holiday in Greece. They're on their way back. We're the only family Aunt Lavender has left."

Rick eyed Johanna. "Are you sure you want to stay here?"

"Yes," she said firmly. "It will give Isaac a chance to get something to eat." She turned to the younger man. "You've been here all night, haven't you?"

Isaac nodded morosely.

"And I'll check on them like I promised," Cunningham assured Rick.

He was still uncomfortable with the situation, but then, he would be until he could make some phone calls regarding Isaac. But if the young man was Johanna's stalker, he couldn't do anything to her here without making a scene.

"Isaac, what all will your aunt need?" Rick said. "I can pack a small bag for her while I'm running my own errands." He scribbled down Isaac's list of toiletries and clothing Mrs. Cresswell would want.

"All right." Rick placed his notebook and pen back in his inner jacket pocket when he finished writing down the items. He eyed Johanna. "I'll be back as soon as I can."

She nodded. Damn, he wanted to pull her into his arms and tell her everything would be all right, but he didn't dare do so in the middle of the ward. Instead, he pivoted on his heel and headed for the stairwell. He needed to run off some of the pent-up energy.

The charge of energy he always got with a good whipping. Now, if only he could convince Johanna to let him remain in her life.

After a shave, a quick shower and a change of clean clothes at his flat, Rick almost felt normal again. He'd checked his back in the bathroom mirror. Maximum pain with minimum damage. He would have compliment Johanna on her technique if it wouldn't anger her.

However, he needed to focus on her case. The emir had been rather alarmed by Rick's account of the last forty-eight hours, though Rick deliberately left out the play session at Club Noir. Also, the emir assured Rick his retainer would be wired into his account immediately along with the expenses of providing new locks at Mrs. Cresswell's Georgian house.

It wasn't the money Rick was concerned about though. He packed two days' worth of outfits and his toiletry case into a duffle bag. With everything ready and sitting by his front door, he sat at his desk in the living room and started on the phone calls he hadn't finished yesterday.

Isaac's supervisor quickly confirmed his whereabouts all day, saying that if the young man had missed a delivery, an angry customer would have rung him. According to Isaac's flatmates, the police met Mrs. Cresswell's nephew on the street as he arrived home from his job. The young man simply didn't have time to attack his aunt, much less change the locks at the Georgian.

That left Johanna's two men from the club.

Rick leaned back in his office chair and tapped his pen against the notepad. Getting information out of the club itself would be next to impossible. However, the butler Colby seemed rather fond of Johanna. Maybe he'd be willing to help if he knew Johanna's safety was at stake.

Ethan Armstong-Home's address was fairly easy to find. However, he couldn't find any listing for Ian Addington in the London metropolitan area. He could be living with someone with an address under their name, a family member, a friend, his latest sub. Johanna's description of him leant toward the abusive type though. Not someone who understood what a real power exchange was.

Rick glanced at the clock. It was already mid-morning and he still needed to go to the hardware shop. He frowned at his notepad again. Something was bothering him about the two former members of the club, but he couldn't for the life of him figure it out.

Less than a half-hour later, Rick wiped his forearm across his forehead before he finished tightening the last screw on the back door lock of the Georgian. So much for getting a shower this morning. The May morning had turned into a bit of a scorcher. At least, he had taken care of the main doors so the bastard wouldn't be waltzing through the house anymore.

He ran up to Johanna's flat to ring Felicity's office and let her know what he'd done. He unlocked the door and pushed it open. No dust trickled down from the top of the door. Worse, the sickly sweet scent of death greeted him. He swallowed bile when he spotted Monica's calico cat lying on its back on Johanna's breakfast table.

Tightening his grip on his tool box, he eased closer. The poor thing had been nailed to the wooden surface and dissected just like the rat had been. Blood had been used to write a message near the cat's head.

you're next, bitch

Chapter Twenty-One

Johanna finally convinced Isaac to go down to the cafeteria for tea and a sandwich. Mister Cunningham reassured the young man he would personally check on both women every ten minutes. Once both men left, Johanna approached the nurse's desk and asked about Mrs. Cresswell's status. Thankfully, the head nurse Mrs. McKinney was a kind soul and handed Johanna the status chart.

She flipped through it, a little relieved Mrs. Cresswell's injuries weren't as bad as she feared. Her landlady did have a nasty concussion along with cuts and scrapes, but she didn't have the cracked skull and severe brain trauma Johanna had feared. She regained consciousness in the ambulance on the way to the hospital, which was a good sign. The nurse on duty during the shift noted Mrs. Cresswell had been awake most of the night, fretting about her tenants and her cat. It explained why she'd been sound asleep when Johanna and her escort arrived this morning.

"Thank you so much," Johanna said as she handed the clipboard back to Mrs. McKinney.

The head nurse shook her head. "I can't believe anyone would hurt a sweet, old lady like Mrs. Cresswell."

"I can't either, But I'm going to find out who did this," Johanna stated before she turned to go back to Mrs. Cresswell's hospital room.

"Doctor Ridgeley?" someone called.

Johanna turned back. Monica strode from the lift and stopped before Johanna. "Is everything all right?"

"Yes." Johanna forced a smile because Mrs. McKinney was taking too much interest in their conversation. "I was just checking on Mrs. Cresswell." She gestured for Monica to walk with her down the hallway.

Monica nodded. "I understand. I checked on her this morning when I got here, too." She glanced around to if anyone else was close before she whispered, "Did anything else happen after you two dropped me off at the bus stop?"

Johanna pursed her lips, not wanting to scare the young nurse, but it was better she knew the truth. "Felicity ran into my harasser. He was coming out of the house as she arrived home from work."

Monica's eyes widened. "Is she all right?"

Johanna nodded. "He didn't do anything to her. He played it off as if he were the locksmith. He probably wasn't sure when you, Rick, and I would be back, so he left."

Monica gasped. "We need to change those locks ourselves. I have some money—"

Johanna held up her hand. "Don't worry about it. It's being taken care of as we speak. Rick will bring your keys here before you leave the hospital this evening."

"You're a good person, Johanna." Monica gave her a shy smile.

"I just want us all safe." Johanna stopped in front of Mrs. Cresswell's door. "I promised Isaac I'd stay with her while he got something to eat. I'll come find you with your keys when Rick comes back."

"Thanks," Monica said brightly before she continued down the hall.

When Johanna entered the hospital room, Mrs. Cresswell was still sound asleep. If she couldn't work, she might as well be studying if she wanted to pass her examinations at the Royal College. She retrieved her notes from her tote bag and began reviewing them.

Johanna checked her watch and stretched. It was well past noon and no word from Rick yet. Not that she really expected it. He had quite a few errands to run, and he might have stopped for a bite since they hadn't had any breakfast.

Isaac snored softly in the other visitor's chair. She'd tried to persuade him to go home and get some sleep, but he refused to leave until his parents arrived at the hospital. The young man was also assuming his parents managed to snag last minute tickets from Greece. Or they could be trapped at another airport if they missed their connecting flight.

Her chair creaked as she stood, and Isaac jerked awake.

"It's all right," Johanna soothed. "I just need to stretch my legs."

He nodded and settled back in his own chair. Soft snores followed her out the door.

She started walking toward the waiting room. She needed something stronger than Earl Grey when Mrs. McKinney called out, "Doctor Ridgeley?"

"Yes?"

"You don't have to go all the way down there." The head nurse inclined her head toward the nurses' breakroom. "It's time for my lunch anyway." She glanced at the nurse sitting beside her, who nodded.

"Thank you." Johanna smiled. "I don't think my stomach could handle any more of the waiting room's coffee."

She followed Mrs. McKinney into the breakroom. The head nurse pointed to the neatly lined boxes of tea. "Irish Breakfast will give you a decent kick without ruining your stomach lining."

Johanna made her cup while Mrs. McKinney retrieved her lunch bag from the refrigerator. When they both sat at the little table in the break room, Mrs. McKinney eyed Johanna.

"I hope you'll forgive my nosiness, Doctor Ridgeley, but how do you know Monica Huxley?"

It was impertinent to ask such a personal question, but Johanna's gut said this was important. Like the sense of déjà vu she had yesterday morning when they discovered the vandalism to Rick's convertible.

"We live in the same building." Johanna took a sip of her tea. "May I ask why you're inquiring about her?"

Mrs. McKinney grimaced and laid her sandwich down on its wrapper. "I hoped that you were mentoring the girl." She shook her head. "Monica is sweet, and she knows her duties, but . . ."

"But what?" Johanna prodded.

"She has a hard time taking charge of a situation. When she was in this ward, she'd forget to give patients their pain meds. I would have to stay on top of her. I fear that's the reason she asked for the transfer to the oncology ward."

"When did she transfer wards?" Johanna asked.

Mrs. McKinney shrugged and picked up her sandwich again. "A month ago."

Johanna took another sip of her tea. A month ago. Right about the time she received the first letter from her stalker. And Monica moved into the building a couple of weeks later.

A shiver ran through Johanna. It was only a coincidence, right? It was definitely a man who called her two days ago. She couldn't picture Monica being able to lower and deepen her voice to such a register.

But then, Monica hadn't specified if the person she stayed with last night was a man or a woman.

"Maybe she does need a little guidance and a boost to her self-confidence." Johanna hesitated a moment, but this was the best time to ask since she and Mrs. McKinney were alone. "Is Monica seeing anyone?"

Mrs. McKinney gave her an odd look as she chewed a bite of her sandwich.

Johanna forced a smile. "I have a cousin who recently moved back to London. I thought the two of them might hit it off. But I don't want her to think she has to date my cousin to get ahead at the hospital."

The head nurse nodded and swallowed. "She was seeing a dark-haired, good-looking bloke when she first started working here. She told one of the other nurses a few weeks back her boyfriend had kicked her to the curb because he was going back to his ex. You'd know before I would if she'd found someone new since then."

Johanna gripped her mug to keep her hands from shaking. Mrs. McKinney was the third person to mention a dark-haired man and the second to see him with Monica. Was her harasser using the poor nurse to spy on who came and went from her flat?

And did that mean Monica was part of Johanna's troubles? Or was the nurse an innocent pawn?

Chapter Twenty-Two

Once again, Rick wiped sweat off his brow before he tapped the little cross into the freshly dug soil with the blade of the shovel. He made the cross with scrap wood and nails he found in the garage, along with the spade to bury the poor cat. Monica was going to be devastated when she learned of her pet's demise.

Especially after he had assured the nurse last night Johanna's stalker wouldn't touch the calico.

Attacking Mrs. Cresswell made sense if the bastard was pretending to be the locksmith, and she became suspicious of him. Killing the rat and the calico made absolutely no logical sense. Which meant if Johanna's stalker was a psychopath, it could be anyone.

That put the investigation back to square one.

Rick knocked off the soil clinging to the blade and carried the shovel back to the garage. He was missing something. Something obvious. Maybe it would come to him while he changed the interior locks.

But as much as he wished his subconscious mind would provide an answer, none came. He knelt in front of Felicity's door. Hers was the final lock to change. He had to pick it open as he had Monica's since both ladies had kept possession of their new keys.

No matter. He needed the practice.

The tumblers clicked, and the doorknob smashed into his nose. Stars alternated with black spots in his vision as he fell backwards.

Automatically, Rick curled and rolled with the blow. A figure darted through the doorway, leapt over him, and raced down the stairs.

Rick scrambled to his feet and raced after the person. Whoever it was dressed completely in black, including a knit ski mask.

The locked back door held up Rick's assailant for a moment. He picked up the decorative vase on the corner display stand and tossed it at Rick.

Rick dodged to the side. The vase shattered upon its landing on the hallway floor planks. He hoped Mrs. Cresswell would forgive him. He also hoped the vase wasn't some priceless heirloom.

The intruder reached for the deadbolt latch. Rick grabbed the person's collar and yanked them backwards. The two landed on the hardwood floor and started trading punches.

Well, the person Rick fought definitely wasn't a girl. Not with all that hard muscle under the black clothing. Rick grabbed a ceramic shard and slashed at his opponent's face. The sharp bit sliced open the yarn covering the intruder's left cheek and nicked the skin. Before the other man got the same idea, Rick aimed a knee at his opponent's package, but the intruder's elbow nailed Rick's diaphragm first. Air exploded from his lungs.

His opponent took the opportunity to break free and lunged for the back door. Rick grabbed his assailant's leg. The other man wrenched the deadbolt lever and yanked open the back door.

Rick barely avoided the kick to his head, but the near-miss accomplished his opponent's goal. The other leg slipped from Rick's grasp, and his opponent stumbled out the back door. By the time Rick scrambled to his feet, his assailant was launching himself over the back stone wall.

He couldn't get away. Rick raced to the back gate and jerked it open. He whirled around looking in all directions. There was no one in the alley. No hint of black flipping over the other fences or walls. No dogs barking to indicate an intruder either.

Damn, damn, damn! Rick slammed his fists against the garage door.

He had the bastard in his grasp and lost him. How the hell could he face Johanna when he'd practically let her stalker go?

But if he went chasing the bastard, he might double-back and steal the new keys. Rick went back into the yard and gently closed the back gate. What if Felicity wasn't as innocent as she pretended to be? They only had her word that she went to stay with her sister. What if the lusty solicitor was the one who hated Johanna? Enough that Felicity set her own subs against the good doctor?

Blood dripped onto his shirt as Rick trudged back into the house. The hours were slipping away. He needed to get cleaned up before he had a talk with either Ethan Armstrong-Home or Colby, the butler.

Chapter Twenty-Three

Relief ran through Johanna when Mrs. Cresswell's eyes fluttered open.

The older woman reached up and touched the bandage covering her stitches on her forehead. "Oh, blast it. I was hoping the whole thing was a dream."

"How are you feeling?" Johanna asked.

"A fake locksmith hit me in the head with a wrench," Mrs. Cresswell grumbled. "How do you think I'm feeling?"

"It sounds to me like you're doing just fine." Isaac grinned.

Mrs. Cresswell eyed him up and down. "Are you still wearing the same clothes from yesterday? Have you been here the whole time?"

"He was worried about you," Johanna said as soothingly as she could. "As was I and the other tenants."

Mrs. Cresswell reached for Johanna's hand, and she held it tightly. "Are you girls all right? He didn't harm any of you, did he?"

"No, but Felicity did talk to someone claiming to be the locksmith when he came out of the house as she arrived home last night." Johanna patted the back of Mrs. Cresswell's hand. "He didn't hurt her, and this was after the ambulance left with you. I just need a description of the man who hit you because I think it might be the same person."

"Your stalker, you mean," Mrs. Cresswell said dryly.

"Yes, I'm afraid so." Johanna flipped to a clean page of her notebook and retrieved a pen from her tote bag.

"Shouldn't she be talking to the bobbies first?" Isaac interjected.

"This man has been harassing me and my tenants," Mrs. Cresswell stated firmly. "It may have started with Johanna, but now he's targeting all of us, and I trust Mister Paine to catch him more than I do the police."

She turned to Johanna. "Please tell me none of you stayed in the house last night."

"No." She shook her head. "I hope you don't mind but we used your automobile last night. We took Monica to the bus stop, and yes, we wait-ed to make sure she boarded the safely. She said she was going to a friend's house. We dropped Felicity off at the Tube station. She was going to take that to her sister's house."

"What about you and Rick?" Mrs. Cresswell narrowed her eyes. She didn't miss much, having been a Domme herself at Club Noir.

"We got rooms at a hotel." Johanna hated lying to Mrs. Cresswell, but she didn't want to admit she'd gone to Club Noir with Rick. Not since she'd barely knew him. And definitely not with Isaac in the room.

Mrs. Cresswell must have sensed something because she turned to her nephew. "Isaac, would you mind getting me some cold water?" She grinned. "And sneak me in a bottle of cola."

He shook his head and laughed. "You could have just said you need-ed some girl time, Aunt Lavender." But he rose and kissed his aunt on the forehead before he left her hospital room. "Will fifteen or twenty minutes be sufficient?"

"Yes." Mrs. Cresswell let go of Johanna's hand and waved at the door. "Now, shoo."

Isaac laughed some more and walked out of the room. He seemed more relaxed now that his aunt was awake.

Mrs. Cresswell turned back to Johanna. "Please tell me he didn't call his parents home from their holiday."

"Sorry, I can't," Johanna said. "You know they care about you."

"*Pfft.*" Mrs. Cresswell made a face. "Petunia is just like my sister. Flighty and incapable of making a decision to save her life. Why do you think Isaac is the one who helps me when I need it?"

"This is a little different." Johanna glared at her landlady.

"So different you took a brand-new sub to the club?" Mrs. Cresswell eyed her right back.

"What was my tell?"

Mrs. Cresswell chuckled. "It was the only place you ever felt safe. I'd hoped living in the flat *above* me would break you out of your shell. This wanker who's been harassing you hasn't helped one little bit." She pursed her lips.

"Rick is changing the locks at the house as we speak. All of them," Johanna added when Mrs. Cresswell opened her mouth to ask.

"I trust him more than I do any locksmith in the city right now." Mrs. Cresswell sighed. "Please tell me you found Rick through the club."

"In a way." Johanna's lips quirked. "Faddil decided I needed a body-guard."

"I swear you're the only Domme I know who can stay friends with her former subs."

The muscles in Johanna's neck and shoulders tightened. "Not all of them."

"You did tell Rick about the two men you had problems with at the club, didn't you?" A cross expression filled her landlady's face.

"Yes." Johanna sighed. "I did, but this man could be anyone."

"Maybe." Mrs. Cresswell played with her blanket a moment before she added, "The reason I became suspicious of the fake locksmith was his resemblance to Ian Addington."

"Ian?" Johanna stiffened in her chair. "Are you sure?"

"Not absolutely." She frowned as she tried to remember. "Between the clean-shaven appearance, the extra weight, and my bloody cataracts, I can't be sure. But my suspicions were enough for him to grab his wrench and bash me in the head with it, so I'm sure my attacker is your stalker."

Chapter Twenty-Four

Rick pulled into the drive of the Armstrong-Home Estate. It was a good thing Mrs. Cresswell let him borrow her car. His convertible wouldn't have flown with this type of crowd. But the closer he got to the main house, the more he noticed how run-down and shabby it really was. Not enough money to keep up appearances. The lack of money might explain some of Armstrong-Home's attitude toward Johanna. The peerage who clung to the pre-war belief that any kind of profession soiled their dainty little hands were finding the world changing without them.

He pulled up before the front doors and climbed out of the vehicle. No sound filtered across the grounds other than birdsong. There wasn't even the scent of spring flowers in the air. Had the family abandoned their estate?

Rick jogged up the front steps. No button for a doorbell. The giant rusty knockers indicated such a thing was too modern for the estate house. He banged one of them three times and waited.

The door creaked open, and a butler even older and with less hair than Colby at Club Noir stood there with a supercilious air. "Madam is not taking visitors at this time." He started to close the door, but Rick stuck his left foot across the doorjamb.

"Wait, I'm not here to see the lady of the house. I'm looking for Ethan Armstrong-Home. This is listed as his place of residence."

The wizened butler snorted. "Have you tried looking in the local whorehouse, sir?"

Before Rick could answer, a querulous voice called out, "Who is it, Hubert!"

"A gentleman is looking for Ethan." Hubert pursed his lips, opened the door wider, and gestured for Rick to come in.

"How much does Ethan owe him?" the feminine voice yelled from the sitting room to his right.

Hubert looked at Rick and raised a bushy grey eyebrow.

"This isn't about money," Rick said.

"Ma'am, he says it isn't about—" Hubert started.

"My eyesight may be going, but my hearing's just fine," the woman snapped. "Bring our visitor in here."

"This way, sir." Hubert shuffled into the sitting room. Rick followed.

An elderly woman sat wrapped in a blanket next to the fireplace. A fire burned merrily despite the heat of the day. The scent of lemon oil cleaner didn't totally cover the miasma of illness. Her white hair was wrapped in a neat bun on top of her head, and her wrinkled face was extremely pale except for some age spots marring her forehead and one cheek.

"Mister—" Hubert looked up at Rick.

"Richard Paine, Lady Armstrong-Home," he answered.

She quickly sized up Rick before she spat, "What did the little prick get himself into this time? Knock up another tart?"

"Not to my knowledge, madam," he replied.

"Then why are you here?"

Something said he wasn't going to get far with the dowager by attempting to spare her feelings. "A house owned by Mrs. Lavender Cresswell in London has been broken into multiple times. All of her tenants are women, and she's extremely concerned about their safety. I've been hired to look into the matter."

"And what does Ethan have to do with this?" Lady Armstrong-Home demanded.

"He had a dispute with one of the tenants which put him on my suspect list," Rick said. "This afternoon, I caught the intruder inside one of the flats. The culprit wore a knit ski mask, but I cut him with a piece of broken vase. All I need to do is examine Ethan's skin."

The dowager pursed her lips. "Is that how you got the black eyes and busted nose?"

"Yes, madam."

"It couldn't be my grandson." She made a very unladylike snort. "I have no doubt you would have thrashed him in any fisticuffs." Her tiny pale hand emerged from beneath her blanket. "Hubert, fetch Ethan. Let's settle this matter."

"Yes, ma'am." Hubert bobbed his head and shuffled out of the sitting room.

"Thank you for your cooperation, ma'am," Rick said.

She sniffed. "Is Mrs. Cresswell aware that one of her girls commits vile and unspeakable acts?"

Rick hesitated. "I don't know what Mrs. Cresswell is and is not aware of, ma'am."

Lady Armstrong-Home sniffed again. "How did you find out about the altercation between Ethen and the tenant?"

Again, it seemed best not to lie to the dowager. "The girl in question reluctantly told me in private of her encounter with Ethan."

"Did he rape her?"

Her question threw Rick off. The last thing he wanted to even think about was Johanna helpless and at the mercy of another man.

"To my knowledge, no."

Lady Armstrong-Home chuckled. "That's what I thought."

"Pardon me?"

"He probably tried to force her to do something she didn't want to do, and she beat the snot out of him." The dowager waved her hand dismissively. "She's not going to tell you the total truth because it's not ladylike." She laughed some more.

Rick kept his jaw clamped shut to keep from telling the dowager she'd hit the mark about both Johanna and her grandson.

Footsteps came from the hallway. Hubert entered with a man. Probably late twenties, but it was hard to tell for certain. The ravages of a hard and fast life had taken their toll on him. He wore a soiled t-shirt and equally abused trousers.

"Grandmother, why the hell is Hubert dragging me out of bed?" But it was Rick who Ethan stared at suspiciously.

She ignored his protest. "Ethan, show Mister Paine whatever body part of yours he wishes to see."

"What?" Ethan looked at his grandmother as if she were starkers.

"Just turn towards me so I can see your left cheek," Rick commanded.

The younger man started to unbutton his trousers.

"Just let me see your face," Rick drawled.

Ethan meekly did so, but other than dark stubble, his skin was unblemished.

"Thank you for your cooperation." Rick turned to Lady Armstrong-Home. "I apologize for disrupting your day, madam." He bowed and turned to leave.

"Mister Paine?" the dowager called.

He turned to face her again. "Yes, madam?"

"Tell the tenant she needs to find a man like you." Her eyes glinted as if she knew or suspected the truth.

"I'll pass along your message." Rick nodded politely. "Good day, madam."

Once he was in Mrs. Cresswell's automobile, he crossed Ethan off his list. He tapped his pen against the pad before he tossed them in the passenger seat and twisted the key in the ignition. He was rapidly running out of potential suspects and wasn't a damn bit closer to Johanna's stalker.

So what the hell was he missing? Or had he been right earlier by suspecting the real culprit was Felicity?

Regardless, he needed to get back to the hospital. It was already well into the afternoon and Monica would need her keys. The real question was whether he could talk Johanna into going back to Club Noir tonight.

His cock twitched at the idea. But this wasn't the time to indulge in his own desires. He really wanted to talk to Colby about where to find Ian Addington.

Chapter Twenty-Five

The sigh of relief Johanna started to release when Rick poked his head around the edge of the hospital room door turned to gasp as his swollen nose and the bruising under his eyes registered. "What happened to you?"

"A little run-in with your admirer," he said sourly. He reluctantly filled in the women about his adventures since he'd left the hospital this morning.

"Oh, dear." Mrs. Cresswell covered her mouth, but her eyes twinkled. "I really believed you would fair better against him than I did."

"The bastard caught us both by surprise." Rick started to chuckle but winced instead. "Don't make me laugh. It hurts too much right now."

"Did you go to the ER?" Johanna demanded. She stood and stepped closer to him. "Your nose looks like it's broken."

"No, and it is," Rick said. "I recognized the crack. But the bleeding has stopped, and it's not out of alignment, so I'm fine."

Johanna jammed her fists on her hips. "When you get a medical degree, then you can make the diagnosis. Come along. I'm taking you downstairs to Emergency." She looked at Mrs. Cresswell over her shoulder. "I'll be back."

"Check on Rick's poor nose." Mrs. Cresswell giggled. "I'll be right here."

Johanna led him out of the hospital room. "What really happened, Rick?"

"The bastard was hiding in Felicity's flat," Rick growled.

There was a catch in his voice that wasn't there before. Johanna grabbed his elbow. "Wait a minute. Do you really think Felicity's involved?"

Rick glanced around the hallway. Even though no one was nearby, he lowered his voice. "Given her kink predilection, odds are you somehow crossed at the club. Maybe someone threw her over for you. I don't know. But the fact that he was in there after he—"

An uncomfortable expression crossed Rick's face.

"After he did what?" Johanna demanded.

Rick grimaced and ran his right hand over his hair. "He killed Monica's calico and left it on your kitchen table."

Johanna's stomach twisted around the sandwich from the cafeteria she'd eaten for lunch. "Oh, my god." She clutched her abdomen before she looked up at him. "Please tell me he didn't do the same to—"

"Mrs. Cresswell's cat is fine." Rick rubbed Johanna's back. "At least, she was when I changed the locks on her flat. Do you need to use the facilities? You're a little green."

"No." Johanna collected the shreds of what was left of her dignity and straightened. "I feel responsible for what he's done to my housemates is all."

"It's not your fault." He stopped rubbing her back. She hated to admit she missed his comforting touch. "This is one sick bastard. He's not going to stop."

He touched her on the small of her back, and they continued walking to the lift. "On the plus side, I met your Ethan today. He's definitely not the man I tussled with at the house."

"No cut on his cheek?" she asked.

"No cut."

"The nurses confirmed Isaac stayed all night with Mrs. Cresswell. He

left about a half hour ago to pick up his parents and bring them here."
Johanna frowned when they reached the lift and she pushed the button.
Her suspicion of Monica was ridiculous, but given Rick was looking at
other alternatives, she made up her mind about mentioning it. "There's
something else concerning. If we're looking at a female culprit, we need
to look at Monica as well."

"Monica?" Rick frowned. "She may be an excellent nurse, but she's
too mousy to be a threat."

The doors opened, and they stepped into an empty car.

Johanna looked up at him as the doors slid closed. "And no one would
considered an ex-military man a submissive, hmm?"

His ears practically glowed red at her teasing rebuke. "Very well, Mistress. Your point is taken. But it wasn't a woman who called you two days
ago, and it definitely wasn't a woman I fought at Mrs. Cresswell's house."

"That doesn't mean our real culprit doesn't have a collaborator," Johanna said. "That could be the case with either Felicity or Monica."

"All right, let's assume Monica is behind the harassment." From his
expression, Rick took Johanna's opinion seriously. "What made you consider her?"

Johanna laid out her talk with the head nurse in Mrs. Cresswell's
ward, along with how Monica just happened to show up when events
connected with the stalker occurred.

Rick's jaw worked as he considered her evidence and logic. "But why
would she kill her own cat?"

"You said yourself that whoever is behind this might be a psychopath." Johanna shrugged. "She may have gotten the cat for the express
purpose of killing it."

"I still can't convince you to call the police and report the whole situation to them, can I?" he muttered.

"Are you saying this is beyond your abilities, Mister Paine?" she said.
Johanna knew she shouldn't be teasing him this way, but if she told the
police everything, it could lead to her being kicked out of Club Noir for

breaking their privacy policy. And she was not ready to give up the club despite her two-year break. In fact, the events of the week told her she needed the freedom of that side of her to be complete.

"I can't protect all four of you at the same time," he said. "It's harder if one or more of you is actively working against me."

His answer took her aback, but the doors slid open and people waited to board the lift. Discussing this wasn't an option in front of witnesses. She led him to the ER. He lied and told the admissions nurse that Johanna opened the door as he was about to go out of their apartment building.

"And it took me hours of nagging him to come down here and get checked," Johanna responded. "I'm fairly certain his nose is broken, but you know men."

The admissions nurse chuckled. "Sounds like my husband after he fell off the step ladder and broke his leg."

"I need to find Monica first, and give her the new keys to her flat," Rick grumbled.

Johanna frowned, trying to figure out his game. "Why don't I take care of that while you get your nose checked?"

"Exactly what I was thinking." He fished in his pocket and pulled out a set keys. "If you don't mind, Doctor Ridgeley?"

"Of course." She accepted the plain ring from him.

"Would you mind if we picked up some Colby cheese on the way home, too?" He smiled blandly.

He wasn't suggesting what she thought he was suggesting. Was he? It made sense to ask the night butler at Club Noir about Ian's whereabouts, but it wasn't likely Colby would divulge secrets of the club's clientele. Or was Rick really asking for another session in a playroom?

"I think we can accommodate your craving, darling." She turned to the admissions nurse. "I'll be right back. Don't let him leave. He shouldn't be driving."

"You broke my nose, not my brain," Rick whined.

Johanna laughed and headed back to the lifts. Two minutes later she approached the nurse's station in the oncology ward. The head nurse Mrs. Badger was at the desk. She resembled her namesake from her squat figure to the white streaks in her black hair. Unfortunately, she could be just as vicious.

"I'm looking for Nurse Huxley." Johanna jingled the keys in her hand. "These belong to her."

Mrs. Badger frowned. "She's already left for the day."

"She has?"

"Claimed she wasn't feeling well. She was running a fever." Mrs. Badger's frown deepened, as if she suspected the younger woman had fooled her somehow. "Aren't you supposed to be on leave, Doctor Ridgeley?"

"I was checking on our landlady who was admitted last night." Johanna tried to look as woeful as possible. "We had a break-in at our building, and I told Nurse Huxley I'd make sure to deliver the new keys to her before her shift ended."

"I don't know what to tell you, Doctor," Mrs. Badger snapped. "She left here shortly after noon."

"Doctor Ridgeley! What are you doing here?"

Johanna winced at the alarm in her supervisor's voice. She turned to face Doctor Bennett.

"I was delivering the keys to Nurse Huxley's flat," she said yet again.

He latched onto her elbow and tugged her away from the nurse's station and around the corner. "You need to leave, Johanna."

"I am." She jerked out of his grip. "You don't have to manhandle me."

"I'm sorry," he murmured. "Someone told Doctor Darlington I gave you passing marks in return for—" He glanced up and down the corridor. "—sexual favors. Now, we're both being investigated."

"What?" she growled. "Do you know who?"

"No." He glared at her. "It wasn't your security consultant, was it?"

"No," she snapped back before she lowered her voice. "It was probably the idiot who left that lovely gift in my locker."

"Perhaps, however, you need to go now, Doctor Ridgeley," he said. "Before matters become worse. For both of us." He pivoted and stalked back toward the nurses' station.

Funny. Monica hadn't said a word earlier about feeling unwell, nor did she appear to be sick. It was all too easy to fake a fever. She'd done it herself to get out of school the year after her mother passed away. And if her harasser was the fake locksmith and Monica's mysterious dark-haired suitor then he would have had the keys to Felicity's flat already.

Johanna strode toward the lift. She needed to get back to Rick so they could plan their next move. Maybe he was right. Maybe they both needed a play session to think clearly.

Chapter Twenty-Six

Pain ricocheted through Rick's eyeballs and right into his brain. He grabbed the ER doctor's wrist. "That's enough poking."

"I'm trying to make sure it's straight so it can heal correctly. You don't want us to have to re-break it to set it properly." The doctor's tone was the same one used when coddling a child. Or calming a madman.

The curtain parted, and Johanna stepped into the bay. Despite the cheerful smile she plastered onto her beautiful face, Rick could see the tension around her eyes and in her neck muscles.

"How are things going in here?" she said brightly.

"Other than Tower Hospital only hires sadists, things are just fine," Rick grumbled.

"Sleep with your head propped up tonight," the ER doctor said. "I can prescribe a painkiller so you can get a good night's rest."

"No," Rick snapped. "I don't need anything."

The ER doctor ignored him and turned to Johanna. "Ice pack every twenty minutes or so to reduce the swelling. OTC painkillers as needed. Call me if he decides he needs something stronger."

"Or she could write the bloody prescription herself," Rick bit out. Pain he could take. This coddling was getting on his last nerve.

The ER doctor looked at Johanna with curiosity.

"Johanna Ridgeley." She held out her palm. "I did my ER rotation a few months ago."

"Ah," he said as he shook her hand. "Where are you assigned now?"

The pulsing behind Rick's eyeballs increased to a pounding, but before he could say anything, someone pushed back the curtain to his bay once again.

"She's supposed to be on leave," Doctor Darlington scolded. "Didn't I tell you to leave Tower Hospital this morning?"

"You said I was on leave from my duties, sir," she replied icily. "This is personal business."

"Not when it involves my hospital," Doctor Darlington roared.

"She wasn't treating my patient, sir," the ER doctor said.

"Do you know she was the one who broke his nose?" The hospital administrator glared at the younger man, who didn't flinch, before Doctor Darlington turned his evil gaze on Johanna. "I also know you've been hiding in another ward all day."

"I wasn't hiding—" Johanna started to protest.

"You are suspended, pending a review of your behavior at Tower!" Doctor Darlington yelled.

That was the last straw. Rick hopped down from the gurney and went nose to broken nose with the administrator.

"How dare you. You apologize this instant," he growled at the older man.

"You have no say—"

Rick didn't take his eyes from Doctor Darlington while he pointed in Johanna's direction. "This woman has been repeatedly harassed at this hospital. She ignored it, knowing she wouldn't get any backing from her superiors. And now, I'm beginning to suspect I was looking at the wrong culprit."

"Rick, stop," she ordered.

"Yes, Rick," Doctor Darlington sneered. "Stop while you're behind."

Rick clenched his fists. Damn, he wanted to deck the bastard, but he could hear Jamie lecturing him in the back of his mind about the different ways one could take down a wanker like Darlington. He took a deep breath and relaxed his fingers.

The hospital administrator seemed satisfied he apparently bullied Rick into submission, so he turned to Johanna. "As for you, Doctor Ridgeley, the hospital board will contact you about scheduling your hearing." He whirled, his long white coat flaring behind him and stomped away.

The ER doctor made a face. "Well, that's a kick in the old twig and berries."

Rick glanced at Johanna as they drove towards her flat. Her normally expressive face was as still as a marble statue of Aphrodite.

Luckily, Isaac had returned to the hospital with his parents. They promised to watch after Mrs. Cresswell at their home for the next few days after their aunt was released from the hospital tomorrow. Mrs. Cresswell's doctor wanted to keep her for observation for another night after the blow to the head because of her age.

Johanna had been perfectly mannered with her landlady's family. She was even straight forward regarding the events that resulted in Mrs. Cresswell's and Rick's injuries, and she offered to feed the cat until they could pick her up tomorrow. Mrs. Cresswell also restated that Rick could use her car while his convertible was in the shop, and gave him the name of the garage where she had his vehicle hauled. But once Rick and Johanna entered the parking garage, she turned silent as the ancient Pyramids of Giza.

Annette hated him interrupting when she was analyzing something quietly. However, it wasn't fair to expect Johanna to act exactly like his previous Domme either, but the quiet was beginning to bother him.

"May I ask a question, Mistress?"

She jumped like she'd forgotten he was in the vehicle, too. "What?"

Her voice cracked on the word, and she cleared her throat. "What did you wish to ask?"

"What are your expectations outside of a scene? You mentioned you normally go over your procedures prior to establishing a relationship."

In his peripheral vision, he noticed her eyes narrowing. "Do you believe this is a relationship, Rick?"

He definitely touched a nerve with that one. But if she was going to demand honesty, then he'd definitely deliver. "Yes, ma'am. I do."

"And you believe you dictate the terms?" she snapped.

"No, not all of them, ma'am." Rick's heart thumped in his chest. She hadn't said they weren't in a relationship, which was a good sign. "However, we haven't had the conversation you mentioned, but that's only because the fecking wanker after you hasn't given us a moment for you to tell me all your rules or ask about my hard limits."

Johanna didn't say anything. He glanced at her again. She had that same faraway look as before.

"Mistress?"

His voice jerked her out of her reverie. "It was a mistake for us to have a scene together given the current circumstances," she muttered.

"Probably," Rick admitted. "That doesn't mean we're not compatible."

"We barely know each other," she scoffed.

"I know you well enough to understand you're angry and upset your integrity has been questioned."

"I would think you're also smart enough to know that having a scene when I am furious is unwise," she answered quietly. At least, she was admitting her real emotional state.

"Yes, ma'am, I do."

"Then what exactly are you expecting here?" She sounded genuinely curious instead of angry.

"That I'm here to listen if that's what you need, Mistress." But he could feel her glaring at him.

"No, I mean why do you really want to go to the club tonight?"

"Two reasons," he said as he made the left turn onto her flat's street. "First, I'm hoping to leverage Colby's affection for you into a last known address for Addington. Second, the club's the safest place for you to stay for now."

"There's something I forgot to tell you while Darlington was dressing me down," she said. "Monica left the hospital early. She told the head nurse of our ward that she wasn't feeling well. Mrs. Badger did say Monica seemed to be running a temperature."

"'Seemed to be'?" Rick glanced at Johanna as he signaled to turn into the alley.

"I had the impression Mrs. Badger thought Monica was faking the fever," Johanna said.

"But Monica knew I was bringing the keys." Rick hit the button for the garage door opener. "When did she leave?"

"Mrs. Badger said shortly after noon," Johanna replied.

Rick hit the brake more sharply than he intended. Both he and Johanna were thrown forward at the sudden stop. He turned and stared at her. "That was around the time I had my little tussle with our intruder."

Johanna stared back at him. "Then where the hell has she been all day if we've had her keys?"

Chapter Twenty-Seven

A shudder ran through Johanna. The timeline made Monica's behavior even more weird and creepy. She stared out the windscreen, trying to think, while Rick parked the automobile properly. What could she have possibly done to cross Monica Huxley?

None of this made any sense. Unless . . .

"Could Monica be the one causing trouble with the hospital administrator?" she mused.

"Possibly," Rick said as he turned off the ignition. "Maybe this has absolutely nothing to do with Club Noir."

"But the letters—" Johanna shook her head. "Is all of this mess because she has a crush on me?"

Rick shrugged. "It's possible. However, she definitely has a partner. It was no petite girl I wrestled with in the downstairs hallway. Let's pack you a bag for tonight."

"What about Felicity?" Johanna asked.

"I could make omelets—"

"No, thank you," she said with another shudder. "Thank to the rat you stored in there, I'm going to have to disinfect my refrigerator thoroughly before I put any food inside."

"What do you suggest while we wait for Felicity?" he asked.

"Have you totally written her off as a suspect?"

"No," he admitted.

"But you've changed all the locks, including the front and back door, right?" she asked.

"Yes."

"Then let's pick up something to eat while we wait for Felicity," Johanna said. "If something happens and Monica doesn't have her keys, we will know for sure."

Rick nodded. "It's a sound plan. Where do you want to go for dinner?"

With all the stress of the week, Johanna asked to go to one of the American fast food places that seemed to grow like mushrooms in London these days. Their food wasn't the healthiest, but she loved their skinny, greasy chips. And if she was going to lose her position at Tower Hospital after all her hard work, she needed something to drown her sorrows.

Rick placed their order to go. She was a little surprised he didn't protest her choice, considering he kept himself in excellent physical condition. Just the memory of last night's sex made her wonder if staying at Club Noir tonight was such a good idea. The insinuation was he would be staying with her.

As they climbed the steps to her flat, Rick said, "The vase that stood by the back door? That wasn't an heirloom of Mrs. Cresswell's, was it?"

"Oh, heavens, no!" Johanna chuckled. "We found that at a flea market three or four years ago."

"We?" But Rick's right eyebrow waggled in a teasing manner.

"Mrs. Cresswell and me," she said tartly.

"I had to ask." He grinned at her and handed her the food before he unlocked her door. A bit of his fingerprint dust wafted down, and she kept the paper sack rolled tight to keep the blasted stuff from getting on her chips.

"Of course, you did." She set her tote bag and purse on the chair that matched her couch while Rick carried their dinner to her kitchen table.

She crossed to the refrigerator. "Did you want some mayonnaise for your fries?"

"I thought you weren't going to eat anything out of the refrigerator until you disinfected it?"

"I hope you disinfected my table after this morning's discovery," she said sourly.

"Twice," he affirmed while he spread out napkins on her table.

"My mayonnaise is sealed, so I'm taking the chance. I can't dip my chips in ketchup."

"Can't or won't?" he teased.

"Both," Johanna retorted as she opened the refrigerator. She closed her eyes and opened them again to affirm what they were telling her. "Rick?"

"Yes, Mistress?"

"What did you do with the rat?"

"It should still be there." Rick stepped closer and bent to look inside. "What the hell?"

The dead rat was definitely missing.

Chapter Twenty-Eight

Rick straightened and scrubbed his hands down his face. Johanna started pulling things from the refrigerator and tossing them in her rubbish bin. He didn't blame her. He wouldn't trust any of the food or condiments either. God knew what Monica and her man had done to them.

"Why don't you leave that until later?" he murmured. "Let's clean up and eat before our food gets too cold. I'll watch for Felicity while you change and pack a bag."

Johanna closed the refrigerator, but she stayed quiet.

"Would you like me to get some fresh mayonnaise at the market?" he asked.

"No." She released a deep breath. "No, thank you. I'm—" She sagged against the refrigerator door. "For once in my life, I'm not sure what I am. I thought being a professional dominatrix was a means to pay for my university and medical school. I love what I did at Club Noir, but the dream of being a doctor was one I had since my mother died. I believed I'd return to the club on a regular basis once I'd passed all my exams, and I became a registrar. If I get kicked out of the medical programme at Tower now, it was all for nothing." She looked up at him. "So, why is part of me relieved?"

"Because you didn't give up on one of your dreams," Rick said. "It was sabotaged. And it means you could go back to a life you found far more satisfying than you originally thought it could be. If you want."

It would also mean he wouldn't be her only sub. His own heart cracked, but her happiness was more important. Watching her work on the injured and unconscious Mrs. Cresswell yesterday afternoon showed him what a damn good doctor Johanna was. And if she remained a doctor, she wouldn't have time for anything else for another year. Could he wait for her? Would she even want someone like him once she was a registrar?

"What I want?" A self-deprecating laugh spilled from her, and she shook her head. "What I want is some food and a good night's sleep so I can figure out what it is I do want in life."

"Then let's take this one step at a time." Rick grinned. "I could run downstairs and see if Mrs. Cresswell has any mayonnaise."

"That's awful." Johanna hesitated a moment. "Do it. I'll repay her with a new jar."

"Your wish is my command." He bowed.

She erupted with real laughter, which sent a pleased feeling through him. He'd lightened his Domme's mood.

His Domme. Johanna made no secret he would be dismissed once her stalker or stalkers were caught. But for now, he'd take any inroad to her heart.

"Oh, Rick, would you please check the cat's food and litter box while you're down there?"

"Of course, Mistress."

Rick watched Johanna swirl her last chip through the mayonnaise on her plate when her phone rang. They exchanged looks.

"Let me answer it this time," he said.

Johanna must have been shaken by the day's events more than he realized. She merely nodded her head.

He stood, crossed to the living room, and grabbed the receiver from its cradle. "Hello?"

"Rick? It's Felicity."

"Are you at the pub? We can—"

"Have you caught the wanker breaking into our house yet?"

"No," he replied as he looked at Johanna. "Not yet."

Felicity sighed. "Given the circumstances, I promised my parents I would stay at my sister's flat tonight. She told them everything, and now they're crawling up my arse about moving home."

"That's actually not a bad idea—" he started.

"No!" Felicity screeched. "Living with my parents is a horrible idea."

"I meant for tonight." He couldn't help grinning at the solicitor's reaction. He had the same feeling when his gran had insisted he move back in with her after his discharge from the army. "I'm taking Doctor Ridgeley some place safe tonight as well. Why don't we drop off your keys at your office tomorrow?"

"That would be marvelous," Felicity gushed. "You two have a good evening. And don't do anything I wouldn't do."

Rick still chuckled when he ended the call. But no sooner than he returned the phone to its cradle, it rang again.

"Please don't let her be offering another chance at a threesome," he muttered. He picked up the receiver again. "Hello?"

"Stay away from Johanna, and I won't kill you." There was a click, and the buzz of a dead line followed.

"It was him, wasn't it?" Johanna scowled, but her emotion wasn't directed at Rick.

"Yes." Rick replaced the phone to its cradle. "He's decided to up the ante from dead cats to dead humans."

Johanna shredded the paper napkin in her hand. "He threatened to kill me?"

"No." Rick returned to the table and sat. "Me."

Chapter Twenty-Nine

Johanna stared at Rick. "How can you be taking this so lightly?"

"It's hardly the first death threat I've ever received." He said the words so calmly it bothered her.

"You are not dying because of me," she spat. "You should leave." Just the thought of losing him in such an obscene manner sent a spasm through her.

"I am not leaving." His brow furrowed. "And I'm certainly not leaving you at his or her mercy."

"It was a man's voice again?"

"Yes." Rick began gathering the hamburger wrappers and chip cartons. "They're hoping to scare me off so they have free access to you." He paused and eyed her. "That is not going to happen."

"You're making this personal," she said.

"Not me. They did when they desecrated my classic convertible." He rose and tossed the wrappers into the rubbish bin.

Another wrinkle in Rick's plans twisted her stomach. "But what about the hospital board?" she protested. "They could call at any time."

He cocked his head and crossed his arms. "You're a physician. Surely you have call forwarding or a beeper in this day and age."

"I do." She matched his pose. "You want to go back to Club Noir so badly you'll risk your life?"

He stepped closer to her, but he didn't touch her. "You're a woman worth taking those risks, Mistress."

With any other sub she had, there was never this intensity of service in either the playroom or outside of a session. Rick was . . . different. Like the knights of old who would serve and protect their queen no matter the cost.

She wiped away the daydreams from her childhood. They were ridiculous anyway. She needed to focus on the real world.

"Unfortunately, you're right," she said. "Club Noir will be safer for both us for the night. If we're not waiting for Felicity, we should leave now."

Luckily, things were slow at Club Noir when they arrived. Upon them entering the main doors, a slight smile tilted Colby's mouth. "Two nights in a row, Mistress Johanna? What a pleasant surprise."

"I am afraid this visit is not a social one," she said. "I need to speak to the Master of the House."

Colby's expression fell. "May I ask to what this is pertaining, Mistress?"

"I'm not sure if it's a personal affair that has spilled into the club, or a club affair that has spilled into my personal life." She regarded Colby for a long moment. "Either way it needs to be rectified for all our sakes."

"I see." Colby rang his little bell. One of the house girls came out, and he whispered to her.

She nodded before she turned to Johanna. "This way, Mistress."

This time, they were led to one of the sitting rooms on the first floor. Once they were alone, Johanna paced. She so rarely had to pull rank at the club, but given the escalating circumstances, the club directors needed to know what was happening. If they blamed her, she would be dismissed. She'd have nothing and no one in her life.

Unless Rick . . .

No, as much as she wanted him, she couldn't let him fall in disgrace with her.

"Mistress, who is the Master of the House?"

"Whichever director of the club happens to be on duty." She shrugged. "There's always a director here. From Colby's expression, more than one of them is at the club tonight. So he needs to summon them all."

"The more people that know—" Rick began.

"Privacy is practically worshipped here," she said. "If someone crosses the line, the directors need to know."

He stepped in front of her to stop her pacing. "What if it is one of the directors who's behind this?"

"What if one of our directors is behind what, Mister Paine?" Colby entered the room along with two other directors she was acquainted with.

If the situation wasn't so serious, Johanna would have thoroughly enjoyed Rick's confused expression.

"Lady Beckworth and Mister Higgins, I present Mister Richard Paine." A bit of a smile tugged at the corners of her mouth. "Rick, I believe you already have met Lord Beckworth."

Chapter Thirty

Rick swallowed his irritation with Johanna and examined the three directors. Lady Beckworth was in her sixties from the loose skin at her neck. Her dark hair had been artfully dyed so the grey streaks accentuated her appearance. She wore a tasteful evening dress and modest makeup, and so she could be any matron out to dinner.

Mister Higgins appeared to be of Nigerian descent from his skin tone and the colorful embroidery decorating his shirt beneath his sports jacket. He was at the indescribable age between thirty and fifty-five. His dark eyes seemed to shine with amusement at Rick's uncomfortableness.

Colby, however, openly grinned at him. "Not what you were expecting, Mister Paine?"

"Not really." Rick cocked his head. "Is Colby your given name?"

"Colby's a cheese, Mister Paine." The man also known as Lord Beckworth shrugged. "My wife gives all her subs the names of cheeses."

Rick swallowed his uncomfortableness. No wonder Johanna gave him an odd look when he mentioned picking up Colby cheese at the market.

"My predilections are not the reason we are here." Lady Beckworth crossed the room and embraced Johanna. "Darling, I know you. You wouldn't ask for a meeting unless the circumstances were dire. Have a seat."

Once the ladies settled on the settee and the men took the remaining chairs, Lady Beckworth demanded, "Now, what the devil is going on?"

Johanna spilled her side of the story from the letters and the emir's hiring of Rick to the sordid confrontation with Doctor Darlington in the ER. Then she indicated for Rick to speak. He added the results of his investigation, the events of the day, and the people left on his suspect list.

Mister Higgins steepled his fingers. "Johanna, I do wish you and Faddil had informed us of the issue with the letters when the first one arrived."

Rick jumped in at the rebuke. "They abided by the club's rules concerning privacy. They were both reluctant to divulge information regarding the club and the nature of their relationship to me."

"The club's privacy was compromised by the directors not nipping this in the bud before it escalated to dead animals and injuries to Lavender," Mister Higgins replied calmly.

"We'll deal with Darlington." Lady Beckworth patted Johanna's hand. "Don't you fret about that little piker. These two women though? I don't recognize the names."

"They could have used false identification," Lord Beckworth said.

"But I thought no one could get into the club without a sponsor?" Rick asked.

"That doesn't mean the women didn't lie about their identities to their sponsor," Lady Beckworth said.

"What about Ian Addington?" Rick asked. "He was the only suspect I haven't been able to locate. Does anyone here know his current whereabouts?"

"I can give you his last known address we have." Lord Beckworth shook his head. "But he disappeared out from under our own investigators' noses at the start of the year."

"Wait." Rick waved his hand. "The club has its own investigators?"

"Yes," Mister Higgins said. "I am one of them. The directors have found it's necessary to keep track of some former members. Addington was a troublemaker from the beginning." He stroked his beard. "He was actually on probation for his poor behavior before he was caught striking Johanna. He also spent some time in prison for beating another woman six months after he was dismissed from the club." He eyed Rick. "I'll pull the photographs of Addington and the female members for you to review."

Lord Beckworth frowned. "Are you really going to let him peruse our files?"

Mister Higgins cocked his head. "Are you questioning Faddil's integrity in hiring this young man?"

"No." Lord Beckworth exhaled gustily. "Blasted politics make everything so much harder than they have to be."

"Faddil and Johanna were right to believe he was the real target of these awful shenanigans," Lady Beckworth said crossly. "A scandal involving him would have a terrible impact with what's going on in the Middle East right now."

"I was not disputing their assumptions, my dear," her husband said. "I probably would have made the same ones in the same situation."

"Very well, then," Lady Beckworth said primly. "Johanna and I will discuss some matters over tea and decadent chocolate dessert while you gentlemen do your detecting."

"Come with me, Mister Paine." Mister Higgins rose and gestured for Rick to follow him.

Rick glanced at Johanna, who gave him a slight nod. Good. The last thing he wanted to do was leave her alone with people she didn't trust. But then, she'd said more than once that Club Noir was where she felt the safest. He and Mister Higgins exited the sitting room and strode down the hallway.

"The privacy aspect doesn't mean you can't ask some questions." Mister Higgins glanced at him with a gleam in his eye. "And I must say, anyone who can attract the attention of the lovely Mistress Johanna is a man to be reckoned with."

"Is that so?" Rick murmured. There were a ton of questions he didn't want to know the answer to.

"For the record, I am not a sub," Mister Higgins said. "You have nothing to worry about from me in regards to Mistress Johanna."

"Is that so?" Rick repeated.

Mister Higgins chuckled. "It sounds like the two of you haven't had 'the talk' yet."

"No time," Rick said. "The bastard stepped up his game once he saw I was in the picture."

Mister Higgins stopped in front of a door that looked like all the other doors Rick had seen in his previous visit to the club. The director unlocked the door.

A younger man seated at a large desk looked up from a computer screen as Mister Higgins and Rick entered.

"Any problems, Mister Dixon?" Mister Higgins asked as he strode past the younger man's desk.

"None so far," Dixon reported crisply. From his bearing, he had either police or military training.

"Very well," Mister Higgins replied. "Carry on."

Rick followed Mister Higgins to an inner office. The director unlocked this door as well, flipped on the lights, and led Rick inside before he closed the door again. The room was incredibly neat and tidy. No paperwork lay stacked on the single desk, only a nameplate that read "Chibundu Higgins". Rows of filing cabinets covered one long wall to the left. Pine cleaner lingered in the air.

Mister Higgins gestured at one of the dark wood chairs with red leather padding on the seat and back. "Have a seat while I retrieve the photo albums for the last two decades."

Rick did as he was told while Mister Higgins unlocked the closet door on the right wall. He returned with two large books easily a meter long and equally wide.

"You handle all of the club's security," Rick asked.

Mister Higgins snorted. "What? You'd think the lords and ladies here would sully their hands?"

"If it satisfied certain urges, they would." Rick smiled.

Mister Higgins roared with laughter. "I like you, Richard Paine."

"It's Rick," he said automatically.

"Chibundu," the other man supplied. He laid a hand on the top book. "I need you to understand if you see anyone you might know, the knowledge cannot leave this room. You are not a member, and I could get my arse kicked to the curb."

Rick cocked his head. "You don't trust Lord and Lady Beckworth?"

"Only to a point." Chibundu shrugged. "Classism still runs rampant in the U.K. It's why Little Lord Armstrong-Home thought he could get away with abusing Mistress Johanna."

"Does Addington have a title?"

"No, but he is the son of the president of one of the major banks." Chibundu chuckled, but the sound had a bitter edge. "New money, old attitude."

He opened the book and flipped to a particular page before he turn the book so Rick could see the pictures right-side-up.

Rick grimaced as he examined the photograph of Ian Addington. So Johanna had a type. Addington and Armstrong-Home could have been related. Similar pouty faces and dark eyes. Lean build. The only thing he had in common with either of them was his dark hair.

"Have you seen him?" Mister Higgins prodded.

Rick shook his head. "He resembles Ethan Armstrong-Home a great deal though. However, he could also fit the description the bartender at the Golden Boar gave us of a man seen with one of the other women living in the same house as Johanna."

Chibundu set the first book to the side and opened the second one. "Let's start with the newer members and work our way back. If Addington is using another member to get back at Mistress Johanna, it wouldn't be any of the members who joined before him." He turned the huge tome toward Rick so he could page through it.

"Who sponsored him though? Surely they'd be embarrassed at his dismissal," Rick said as he began scanning the photographs.

"Lady Beckworth wasn't embarrassed." Chibundu chuckled. "She was infuriated by her stepson's behavior."

"Stepson?" Rick's head jerked up at that bit of information.

Again, Chibundu shrugged. "From her first marriage to said bank president. She thought she was helping Ian discipline his violent urges. After he ended up in prison for nearly beating his girlfriend to death, his father disowned him. Lady Beckworth's guilt over Ian's actions is one of the reasons she dotes over Mistress Johanna."

"You lost track of Addington after he was released from prison," Rick stated.

"Yes," Chibundu admitted.

Rick started flipping through the pages as he let that information digest. A good-looking man down on his luck? He could see how Addington would rope women into providing him a place to stay.

"What was his girlfriend's name?" He looked up at Chibundu. "The one he almost beat to death?"

The director frowned. "Let me pull his file and check." He rose and stalked over to the last filing cabinet. Chibundu unlocked the top drawer, pulled out a file folder, and brought it back to his desk.

He flipped through the contents before he pulled out a stapled sheaf and slid it across the desk to Rick. "The police report."

Rick examined the intake information, but nothing rang a bell. He flipped to the page with the victim photos. The brutality was one thing, but it was the woman's face that sent a stab of worry through his stomach. She could have been an older version of Monica Huxley.

Chapter Thirty-One

Rick re-read the intake report. There it was. The victim Alice Huck-lebee had a teenage daughter, Miranda.

Which would make her around the same age as the woman he knew as Monica Huxley.

Hucklebee caught Addington having sex with her daughter. When she confronted him, he beat her so badly she ended up in critical care. A neighbor was the one who called the police after hearing the incident through the thin walls of their flats. Miranda refused to cooperate with police, saying she loved Addington.

"What is it?" Chibundu asked.

Rick turned back to the picture of the victim and handed the sheaf to the director. "This woman may be the mother of one of Johanna's neigh-bors." He repeated his assessment to Chibundu, who nodded thought-fully.

"It makes sense. Mistress Johanna wasn't much older herself when he first brought her here. However, he underestimated her mental strength. He was never going to turn her into a submissive."

"So, he figures he'll start with someone younger," Rick added. "While she's still mentally moldable." Another thought struck home. "When did Lavender Cresswell stop coming to the club?"

"Lavender Cresswell?"

"She is Johanna's landlady," Rick said. "She already told me that's how she and Johanna became acquainted. She also said the fake locksmith had a passing resemblance to Addington. If it were him, she's damn lucky she's alive."

"Mistress Lavender was a director before her retirement. Let me make some phone calls," Chibundu said. "This situation will not end well if Addington and his accomplice are not caught. And quickly."

Rick continued to look through the Club Noir member albums while Chibundu called a friend at Scotland Yard and two other people. Rick couldn't catch a word of the second and third calls because Chibundu spoke Nigerian. In each case, the director faxed the photograph of Alice Hucklebee. When he returned the receiver to the cradle, he looked at Rick with a grim expression.

"Alice Hucklebee disappeared three months ago. Her employer made the report when she didn't show up to work.

"February?" Rick breathed. "The month after Addington was released from prison."

"And my contact at the prison confirmed that a young woman resembling Hucklebee picked up Addington on the morning of his release. The license plates and car belonged to Hucklebee."

"Would it be acceptable if you went with me to the apartment building where Alice Hucklebee was last living?" Rick asked.

"I'd call you a fool if you didn't take back up, Rick." Chibundu grinned. "And you don't strike me as a fool, else Faddil would never have hired you."

Rick couldn't relax in the passenger seat of Chibundu's nondescript sedan, even though the director was correct in saying they should take a vehicle Addington had likely never seen.

"You a definitely a paradox, my friend," Chibundu commented as they sped across the city.

"I beg your pardon?" Rick looked at the director.

"You have no problem submitting to Mistress Johanna, but you keep pressing your imaginary accelerator." Chibundu chuckled.

Rick had to laugh, too. "My corporal had a similar complaint."

Chibundu signaled a left turn and pulled into the entrance of a council estate. Even in the dark, Rick could tell it was in much better shape than the estate where he'd been raised. They exited the automobile and headed for the flat matching Alice Huckabee's address.

Music and laughter filtered through the common car park. The odors of various ethnic cuisines mixed as well. Some residents peeked around their curtains while others sat on concrete half-walls smoking and joking. The men and teenagers outside glanced at Rick and Chibundu with curiosity before returning to their own conversations.

Chibundu knocked on the door. A very pregnant young woman opened it.

"Yes?" she said.

"I'm sorry to bother you, but I'm looking for Miranda Hucklebee," Chibundu said with a pleasant smile.

"Don't tell me she nicked from you, too?" The young woman groaned.

Rick and Chibundu exchanged looks.

"She didn't take anything from us," Chibundu said.

"Actually, I have her cat," Rick said. "I wanted to return it."

"Her cat?" The young woman frowned. "Miranda didn't have a cat. At least, not while she was living here."

"Were you roommates?" Rick said. "Because she said she lived here with her mother."

"I think she scammed you, love." The young woman gave him a sad smile. "If it's any consolation, you aren't the first. She moved out to live with her new boyfriend three weeks ago." She started to close the door.

"Wait." Rick pressed against the door. "Would you look at a picture for me? This is important."

"You bobbies?" Her expression turned suspicious.

"No," Rick said. "I'm a private security consultant. Her mother's former boyfriend was released from prison five months ago. He's been harassing women he feels wronged him, including my client." He took the picture Chibundu handed him and held it up for her to see. "Have you seen this man?"

The young woman gasped. "That can't be her mother's boyfriend. That's Monica's boyfriend. Ian. The one she supposedly moved in with."

Chapter Thirty-Two

Hours later, Johanna listened in silence as Mister Higgins relayed his report of his and Rick's investigation this evening. Strings had already been pulled to have Mrs. Cresswell's attack and Alice Hucklebee's missing persons case assigned to a friend of Mister Higgins at Scotland Yard. An APW had been issued to locate Ian and Monica. Given Monica, or rather Miranda, had left the hospital early today, there was a good chance the two would try to leave the country.

"You and Rick will be staying at the club until Ian and Monica were caught," Lady Beckworth declared while she patted Johanna's hand. "This whole situation with Ian and this other girl is totally unacceptable."

Mister Higgins eyed Johanna. "Mistress, did you plan to sponsor Rick's membership to Club Noir?"

"I-uh—" All rational thought seemed to flee from her brain.

"We barely know each other," Rick inserted smoothly. "The only reason I even know about the club is because I insisted on full disclosure from the emir and Mistress Johanna before I accepted the case."

Mister Higgins' grinned showed his white, white teeth. Johanna couldn't remember ever seeing the director in charge of security smile. "Well, then, may I extend the offer of sponsorship? I could use someone like you in our security department."

In response, this was the first time she ever saw Rick appear nervous. "Well, that's very gracious of you—"

Anger surged through her. "I don't appreciate you teasing my sub, Master Chibundu. If you wish to offer him an employment position, then I'll be happy to sponsor his membership. However, in all other matters, he is mine."

"As you wish, Mistress Johanna." Mister Higgins inclined his head.

Inside the normal sleeping quarters a half hour later, nerves assailed Johanna despite the directors' assurances they would assist in rectifying both of her problems. Their promises didn't stop the stress from her worries over her career and the possibility Ian was trying to harm her for her part in him getting kicked out of Club Noir.

It didn't help when Chibundu Higgins tried to lay claim to Rick. Out of all the other Dominants at the club, she never imagined him trying to alpha his way over her. Or did he see her as weak thanks to Ian and Monica's campaign to ruin her life?

No, her real problem would be letting go of Rick when this was all over. Tonight, she should have insisted she and Rick have separate rooms. Even if she desperately wanted to whip him out of her blood, she couldn't be that cruel. His back would still be sore from their play session last night.

"The directors assumed we would spend the night together," Johanna murmured. "I should have insisted on a second room for you."

"Why?" Rick paused in unzipping his bag.

"I took advantage of you last night." She shook her head. "I apologize. That was inexcusable of me."

"I don't recall saying no to anything you wanted to do to me." Rick smiled. "I wanted to be with you, in any capacity, just like I want to be with you tonight."

"This—" Johanna waved her hand between them. "This thing can't be anymore than it is."

"So what is this thing between us?" He closed the space between them, but he didn't touch her. He wouldn't. Not here. Not without permission. "And why can't it be exactly what we want it to be?"

She sighed. Of course, he didn't understand. "Once I return to my position at the hospital, I'm going to have to be on my toes. Darlington will be embarrassed he was overruled about my suspension by the board, even if his decision were absolutely without cause. He'll be looking for an excuse to get rid of me. I won't have time for anything more."

"Has it occurred to you that maybe I like the fact I won't have to babysit you or shop with you or any of the other things women demand of their men?" he growled. He was close enough his body heat seeped from his clothes and penetrated her. "That I like you doing things to me. Things that only you have the strength to do."

"Why are you making this harder for both of us?" She couldn't stop herself. She reached up and traced the curve of his mouth.

"It doesn't have to be hard for either of us, Mistress." He smirked. "Or it could be as hard as you want it to be."

She didn't have to look down to know exactly what he was referring to. "Why do you do this?"

"Do what, Mistress?"

"Tempt me so."

"What if we have vanilla sex tonight then?" he murmured. "If it's plain, it might not be so tempting to you."

Johanna laughed. She couldn't help herself.

"With all due respect, Mistress, a woman laughing at a man is not the gentlest of ways to turn him down." But there was a twinkle in Rick's eyes that said he was silently laughing with her.

"And do you think you'd be in control if we did have vanilla sex?" she asked.

"No, Mistress." The same gentle expression came back to his face. "Never." He knelt in front of her and remained silent.

Indecision tore at the threads of Johanna's own control. Never had

such a strong man so willingly knelt at her feet. He'd do anything to protect her, but never once had he forced her to do anything against her will.
If something was important, he used logic and reason. So why was she
fighting her attraction to him so hard?

Because she was expecting betrayal, she realized with a start. Her relationships with Ian and Ethan resulted in them trying to take control
of her. The rest had been like Faddil, someone who had no interest in a
romantic relationship. They were men she could keep well away from her
heart and still find satisfaction in the domination part of their activities.

Rick was a rarity. He could possibly be both. That's what made him
tantalizing.

Her fingertips lightly pressed his chin, and he lifted his head. There
was no triumph in his expression.

"Here are my rules," she murmured. "Our sessions will be planned
ahead of time from now on. I don't risk my subs well-being through in-
attention or excess negativity that has nothing to do with our play time.

"Do not lie to me for any reason. I do not need protection, and I take
no pleasure in doing things to you that you do not enjoy or find release
from as well. If you are afraid of hurting my feelings, we are ill-suited to
begin with.

"Once the matters with Ian Addington and at the hospital are settled, we will sit down and create a list of your desires, things you wish to
try, and your hard limits. If you ever have a question, do not hesitate to
ask in private. But for the most part, you will not speak unless spoken to.

"Do you have any questions now?"

His Adam's apple bobbed. "No, Mistress."

There wasn't any need for a safe word since no punishments or pain
were involved. But discipline? Discipline was always the most difficult
element for men to master. Tonight would show if she and Rick could be
compatible.

She crossed to the bed and perched on the foot. "Rise. Take off your
clothes, Richard, and fold them neatly."

He stood. A healthy erection already pressed against the zipper of his jeans. He shed his clothes, placing the folded items on top of his suitcase. When he finished, he stood at parade rest, his eyes lowered, and he waited for her next instruction.

"Turn around so your back is facing me," she ordered.

He hesitated for less than a blink of an eye, but he obeyed. Most of his scars were thin slices, but a few were jagged marks.

"Tell me about the scars on your arse and legs," she said.

Once again, he hesitated for a split second before he answered, "They're from a landmine, Mistress."

"You weren't the one who stepped on it, were you?"

"No, Mistress."

"Who did?"

"Minister Wynton-Smythe, Mistress."

Of course. The minister played up his military service record during his campaign, including the loss of his leg.

Johanna stood and crossed to Richard. Her fingers traced the white remnants on his flesh of a stupid war. Goosebumps rose along his skin at her touch.

"You saved his life, didn't you?" she murmured.

"Yes, Mistress."

"What do you owe him that you responded to his request for assistance when the minister called you?"

"He saved my life after we returned from the Falklands." The slightest burr of emotion quivered in Richard's voice. The same emotion when he spoke of his previous Domme.

She closed her eyes and leaned her forehead against the hard muscles of his back. "He kept you sober and sane after your previous Domme shut you out of her life."

Richard said nothing, but then she hadn't asked a question either.

"Turn around and face me, Richard."

He did. The old pain was evident in his face, but so was hope. Hope that she wouldn't cast him aside once Ian was apprehended.

Johanna reached up and stroked his cheek. "Tell me what you need, Richard."

"I need you, Mistress." His voice rasped. "I need to know you feel this connection between us."

She stood on her toes and kissed him. A thorough kiss. But she knew she had to say the words, too.

"I do feel the connection," she whispered into his mouth. "More than you realize." She stared into his deep brown eyes. "But I need to take this slowly. I don't want to be a substitute for your previous Domme when she shattered your heart so completely." She rested her palm on his chest, the rapid thrum telling her his fears and hopes. "I don't want to be the one who breaks you for good. You already know how complicated my past is. I have to learn how to trust you not to break me either."

Relief washed across his face. "I understand, Mistress. May I ask a favor?"

"If I can grant it." She smiled.

"May I touch you and pleasure you? I want to serve you properly."

"Yes."

Rick's fingers trembled a bit when he reached for the buttons of her blouse, but the nervousness faded as she let him undress her. He took his time, carefully removing each item of clothing. Not rushing, he folded each item neatly and stacked it on top of his own pile of clothing.

Her heart fluttered at his symbolic gesture.

Once she was naked, he crossed the room and turned down the covers before he picked her up. Cradling her in his arms, he carried her to the bed and gently placed her on the cool, crisp sheets.

Rick began with butterfly kisses on her lips, her eyelids, the tip of her nose. Johanna closed her eyes. No one had ever treated her with such regard. The feather light touch of his lips was followed by callused fingertips stroking every inch of her. The sensation was relaxing and erotic at the same time.

Her breasts grew heavy and full. His mouth took her right nipple, sucking and nipping until it was a hard bead, before he lavished the same attention on her left. Her fingers stroked his hair and encouraged him.

When his mouth released her left breast, a tiny moan of disappointment escaped her. He kissed and licked his way down her body before he settled between her legs.

Her eyes popped open. "Wait," she murmured. "There's dental dams and condoms in the bedside—"

Rick reached up and lay a finger across her lips. "I haven't been with anyone in nearly eight years. You haven't been with anyone in two. We've already discussed our histories unless there was something you left out."

"No," she murmured. "I'm simply too aware—"

"I trust you." He stared into her eyes. "Now, I want to taste you, Mistress."

The way he spoke sent a rush of warmth and desire through her pelvis. She nodded her permission because her tongue was glued to the roof of her mouth in anticipation of what came next.

The first tentative stroke drew a gasp from her. By the fifth, his hands clamped her hips to keep her writhing from taking away his treat. There was no escape from his talented tongue. It flicked and teased her tiny bud into its own submission. Two of his fingers entered her, adding to the bliss.

She cried out when he drew his head back, but he simply puckered his lips and blew across her tortured flesh. Her pussy spasmed around his fingers, and his mouth caressed her to draw out the exquisite tremors.

"May I continue, Mistress?"

"Continue?" Her thoughts seemed to have shattered with the rest of her.

"Yes, please."

"You may," Johanna said between gasps of air.

He pushed himself upright. His cock bounced jauntily as he lifted her hips.

He thrust his cock into her, and her body definitely wasn't ready to stop. Her internal muscles squeezed him with each stroke.

Rick filled her, complimented her, completed her. Why had she fought so hard over the last three days to get him out of her life?

He stiffened, and the throb of his cock filling her set off the most delicious orgasm. He stroked her belly as she shook. While she panted, he gently withdrew and laid down beside her, his head in the crook of her shoulder.

"You did very well, Richard," she murmured as she stroked his hair. "Very well."

No, she definitely couldn't give him up. After three days, she couldn't imagine life without him.

Chapter Thirty-Three

Rick swung by his flat first to pack his largest suitcase since they weren't sure how long they'd be staying at Club Noir. Before he left the club, Chibundu asked if it was all right to give Rick's number to his detective friend at Scotland Yard. Rick agreed, knowing Chibundu wanted a thorough background check before he made any formal job offer. However, Chibundu surprised Rick by giving him both Chibundu's personal and business numbers as well as both for his detective friend.

Chibundu also suggested Rick forward his calls to the director's direct line at the club. If Rick was unavailable, Chibundu could coordinate if the call was related to Johanna's case, and he could forward any personal calls to voicemail.

Rather than parking in the garage, Rick pulled to a stop in front of Mrs. Cresswell's Georgian. Addington was probably watching the place, but God only knew from which building. Doing something unexpected would hopefully throw him off a bit.

Once inside, Rick's first stop was Mrs. Cresswell's flat. He put out fresh water and food before taking care of the cat's litter box. The puss proceeded to thank him by twining around his legs and leaving a thick layer of white cat hair on his trousers.

It was a good thing he packed his lint brush.

Rick locked up Mrs. Cresswell's place and jogged up the stairs to

Johanna's flat. The door was still secure. He inserted the key, twisted it, and pushed open the door.

His fingerprint powder puffed from the top of the door. Air stirred inside, but he didn't remember Johanna having a fan. The fluttering curtains in the breakfast nook caught his attention.

The window over the little table had been totally smashed out of its frame. Rick turned to check the living room when something smashed into the side of his head. He landed hard on his side. Spots danced in his vision. He rolled on his back, willing the pain to subside.

"I expected a security expert to be a little tougher."

Rick tried to force his eyes to focus. Two men stood over him. No, only one. Addington. And he was armed with an aluminium cricket bat.

"Let's see if our darling Johanna will come to your rescue, little sub." Addington raised the bat over his head.

Rick rolled toward Addington, catching the bastard off guard. He tried to dance out of the way, but Rick hooked his right arm around one of Addington's ankles. The wanker hit the floor, but not without kicking Rick in the head.

Everything greyed in his vision. He couldn't give up. God only knew what horrible things Addington would do to Johanna if he wasn't stopped. Because she would come here if Rick didn't go back to Club Noir in a reasonable time.

He grabbed the leg of the small table by the door and tried to pull himself upright. Nausea roiled, threatening to spill not just his breakfast, but all his internal organs as well. On his feet already, Addington swung the illegal cricket bat.

Rick ducked and yanked the table over him. The wood cracked with the blow, but he wasn't able to avoid the backswing. The aluminium bat struck his head in the same place as before.

This time, the blackness enveloped Rick and dragged him into its depths.

Chapter Thirty-Four

Johanna jumped at the harsh ring of the room phone as she sat at the desk and reviewed her notebook. She steeled herself. If it were someone from within the club, they would have sent one of the staff to deliver the message. The members were rather old-fashioned that way.

She picked up the receiver. "Hello?"

"Is this Doctor Ridgeley?"

"Yes, it is. To whom am I speaking?"

"This is Mrs. Gardner, Doctor Darlington's assistant at Tower Hospital."

Ah, yes, his cranky secretary. Of course, he wouldn't bother to call Johanna himself.

Before she could formulate a reply, Mrs. Gardner said, "Your review before the hospital board is schedule for eleven a.m." The phone call abruptly cut off.

Johanna replaced the receiver and glanced at the clock. Less than an hour. Well, she knew Darlington would pull something like this after one of the board called him to task.

A knock on the door echoed through the room. She gritted her teeth. There was no time for other shenanigans. She needed to change and arrange for transportation. However, she answered the door first.

"Good morning, Mistress Johanna." Lady Beckworth swept into the room along with two staff members. All of them carrying various clothing bags and cosmetic accoutrements.

"The switchboard told you about the call," Johanna said as she closed the door.

"Of course." Lady Beckworth set the two boxes she carried on the desk. "My friend on the board was more than a little vexed over Darlington's behavior." She waved a hand. "But it's time we give him enough rope to hang himself as the saying goes." She made a hurry up motion. "Now come along, girl. Get those clothes off. You can't go to this hearing looking like a ragamuffin."

"But I need to leave now," Johanna protested. "This isn't a party."

"Pish-posh," Lady Beckworth tutted. "You need to look like the accomplished professional woman you are." She directed the other two women while Johanna stripped off her t-shirt and jeans.

The length the director had gone to touched Johanna. "Thank you for your help."

"Don't worry, my dear." Lady Beckworth smiled as she held up a white silk blouse for Johanna to slip into. "I'll make sure Cinderella arrives at the ball on time."

Lady Beckworth was a woman of her word. Johanna exited the limousine with the brand new leather tote beneath her arm and marched into Tower Hospital. Whatever happened at this meeting with the hospital board would settle her medical career once and for all.

Mister Cunningham waited for her at the reception desk with a bit of a smirk on his face. "Good morning, Doctor Ridgeley."

"Mister Cunningham." She nodded.

He fell in step with her as she strode toward the lifts. "Bit of a row on the top floor this morning."

"I can imagine," she replied.

"It's been amusing watching a certain administrator getting taken down a peg or two."

She sighed as they boarded the lift with half a dozen other people. She also prayed Mister Cunningham would remain silent about the imminent review on the ride up to the top floor. Thankfully, he did.

They were the only two left in the car when the doors opened in the administration section. Mrs. Gardner stood in front of the lift, a scowl on her face.

"This way," she snapped before she turned and marched toward the conference room.

Johanna had only been up here once for last year's Christmas party. The view of the city was as spectacular as it had been five months ago. The frowning faces of Doctor Darlington and the board members were less spectacular.

Doctor Bennett was in attendance as well. There was one empty chair beside him. Mister Cunningham claimed the other empty chair beside Mrs. Wainwright, the board secretary.

Sir Douglas Chatham, the president of the Tower Hospital Board, gestured toward the chair by Bennett. "Please have a seat, Doctor Ridgeley."

She strode to the chair and sat, but she kept her face impassive and her head high. She couldn't back down or be seen as weak.

"We've been discussing the matter of your suspension," Sir Chatham said. "Doctor Bennett says there has been no problem with your performance. Doctor Darlington has made some rather unseemly accusations. Furthermore, the head of security Mister Cunningham has informed us of some disturbing incidents targeted toward you. Is there anything you'd like to say before we begin?"

"Only that my work speaks for itself." Johanna gripped the arms of the chair tightly to quell her temper. "And Mister Cunningham has lectured me about security protocols within the facility. My efforts to deal with a personal issue spilled into my workplace, and for that, I apologize to both the board and Mister Cunningham."

"Are you and Doctor Bennett seeing each other socially?" Mrs. Wainwright asked. The board's secretary appeared to be displeased by this entire farce.

"No, ma'am, we are not."

"And why would you tell the truth now?" Darlington snorted.

"Why do you listen to employee gossip?" Johanna asked calmly.

"Are you denying it?"

Johanna sighed. "I already have. Not to mention, the nurses' grapevine also says Doctor Oakes is sleeping with Doctor Bennett, which also isn't true."

"For all I know, the three of you are in some sordid relationship—" Darlington started.

"That's enough!" Bennett barked. "Slander of the medical staff is no way to run a hospital."

"Are you saying you haven't thought about fucking her?" Darlington gestured sharply at Johanna. Most of the board gasped in shock, but Sir Chatham's ears turned bright red.

"You're right, Darlington," Bennett snapped. "I asked her out. I was lonely since my wife left me, and I fucked up. Doctor Ridgeley, very kindly I might add, pointed out that dating her could possibly ruin my career." He looked at her. "If she had said yes, I would have ruined my relationship with my children, and I wouldn't have met a lovely widow at church, whom I'm currently seeing." He turned back to the members of the hospital board. "So, yes, I am sticking up for Doctor Ridgeley because she saved me from myself in the aftermath of my divorce, and she was kind and gracious in doing so."

Johanna blinked. The impassioned speech was so unlike her supervisor's normal detached behavior since she'd turned him down during her first year.

"Mister Cunningham, would you like to add anything to your original statement?" Sir Chatham asked.

"Yes, sir." Cunningham stood. "I was contacted by an Inspector Dunham from Scotland Yard this morning. Apparently, a suspect in another woman's disappearance is the prime suspect in regards to Doctor Ridgeley's stalker." He grunted. "I'm glad you took my advice, and called the police."

She shrugged. "The rat was one thing. Killing my neighbor's cat and leaving it on my kitchen table and beating my landlady were a couple of steps too far. The police have issued an APW."

Johanna's statement triggered appalled expressions from everyone, including Doctor Darlington who exclaimed, "I wasn't told about this!"

"Given the circumstances, you are hereby reinstated at Tower Hospital with commiserate privileges and responsibilities." Sir Chatham glared at Doctor Darlington. "The board has some additional matters to discuss with the hospital administrator and Doctor Bennett." He turned and smiled at Johanna. "That will be all, Doctor Ridgeley. Thank you for coming. We expect you back in the oncology ward tomorrow morning."

Johanna stood and nodded before she turned and left the conference room. She felt sorry for Bennett. He'd put himself in a precarious position by admitting his transgression and for sticking up for her character. She hoped the board would take into consideration he had backed off when she said no and hadn't retaliated against her.

Whatever relief she felt evaporated as she recognized the woman standing by the lifts, obviously waiting for her.

Monica Huxley, AKA Miranda Hucklebee, grinned at her, but the expression was neither friendly nor reassuring.

"I suppose you want your new keys," Johanna said.

"I figure you'll unlock the doors for me."

"And if I choose not to accompany you?" Johanna glared at the woman.

Hucklebee stepped closer. It was all Johanna could do to hold her ground when what she really wanted was to chain Hucklebee and find new ways to inflict pain.

The nurse lowered her voice. "If you don't come with me, your security expert will end up like the rat in your locker."

Chapter Thirty-Five

A little man pounded Rick's skull with a sledge hammer. But Rick couldn't go back to sleep. There was something terribly important he needed to do, but he couldn't move. His shoulders ached, and his toes throbbed.

He forced his eyes open. Even they hurt. The bright sunlight coming from his other side didn't help his aching head one bit.

Johanna. He was in Johanna's flat.

The breeze from the broken window highlighted parts of him that shouldn't be feeling any breeze at all. He carefully looked down.

Yep. Naked as the day he was born. And tied to the wooden kitchen chair he sat on by an expert. None of the rope had any give anywhere.

"Glad you could rejoin me," a male voice rasped. "I'd hate for you to sleep through all the fun."

Rick slowly turned his head. Addington stood on the other side of Johanna's kitchen island. An array of torture items sat on the countertop. Not fun ones either. No, these were the kind he was told about in the service. The kind an enemy used to maim in order to collect information.

"It doesn't matter what you do to me. She's out of your reach," Rick growled.

"Actually, she's on her way here." Addington's expression was sheer malice. "Monica is a very obedient sub. I sent her to get Johanna from the hospital, and Monica will do whatever she has to."

"You mean Miranda?" Rick said.

Addington flinched, but quickly recovered. "So you know. Doesn't matter."

"What did you do with Alice's body?" Rick asked.

This time, pure rage flooded Addington's face. "It's in the same place I'm going to put you and Doctor High-and-Mighty." The anger disappeared to be replaced by anticipation. "I have to thank you for getting rid of any witnesses for me." Addington grinned.

The rapid change in the bastard's moods meant something was profoundly broken in his head.

"Thank you for not killing Mrs. Cresswell," Rick replied.

"The old biddy started asking too many questions," Addington growled. "She acted like she knew me. I just needed her out of the way for a couple of days. But then, you wouldn't leave Johanna alone."

"Well, she did hire me to find you." Rick chuckled despite the pain. He was fairly certain one of his molars was cracked from that damn aluminium bat.

"Did the whore spread her legs for you, too?" Addington spat. In his renewed rage, he didn't wait for an answer. "She pissed me off to get me to hit her. Then, she got me kicked out of my private club so she could fuck all the other men there."

"She would have stayed with you if you hadn't tried to change her into something she's not."

Addington stalked around the island. Even though Rick braced for the blow, the back fist across his cheek hurt like a son of a bitch. Yep, that last molar was definitely cracked.

"I'm not in the mood for waiting for the bitch." Addington reached for one of the culinary blowtorches on the counter. "I need to have some fun now."

Rick tried to make his brain work faster. Find some way out of this. Pain he could deal with, but he couldn't bear to see that hissing blue flame blacken Johanna's soft skin.

Chapter Thirty-Six

Johanna was more than a little shocked when Monica/Miranda pulled up in front of the Georgian and parked behind Mrs. Cresswell's sedan.

Mrs. Cresswell's automobile. Rick was driving it. He was picking up clothing for himself and Johanna before meeting with Inspector Dunham to deliver the evidence they'd collected.

"How did you two get back in the house?" Johanna choked out.

"I can't vouch for that git Felicity." Monica/Miranda motioned for Johanna to get out of the car.

"I meant you and Ian," Johanna said.

That bit of news surprised Monica/Miranda from her initial expression, but she quickly recovered. "So you figured it out. Aren't you a clever girl?"

"Ian is just using you, Miranda."

"Get out, now!" she roared.

Johanna climbed out. For a split second, she considered running down to the Golden Boar to get help. She couldn't take on both Ian and Miranda if Rick was incapacitated. But by the time the police arrived, she had no doubt Rick would be dead.

She swallowed the bile and anger in the back of her throat and unlocked the front door. She eyed Miranda over her shoulder as she pushed open the door. "Did you adopt that calico for the sole purpose of killing it and leaving it in my kitchen?"

"What?" For the first time, Miranda appeared shaken. "What are you talking about? Patches is in my flat."

Johanna sighed. "No. The cat's buried in the back yard under the hawthorn. If you didn't kill it, Ian must have."

"You're lying!" Miranda spat as she followed Johanna inside. "He'd never do anything like that."

"If that's true, then where's your mother?"

"Get upstairs," Miranda ordered. However, she glanced at her own flat's door.

Johanna was fairly certain she saw a flash of guilt on the younger woman's face. At least, she had some remorse. For the cat, if not for her mother.

They climbed the steps without another word. An odd odor lingered in the upstairs hallway, but Johanna put it out of her mind while she unlocked the door to her flat and opened it.

The awful smell of burnt hair filled Johanna's nose before the sight registered. Rick sat naked, tied to one of her kitchen chairs on the rug between the kitchen and living areas. Patches of soot clung to the skin of his chest, arms, and legs.

Ian shot her an ugly smile. "Just in time for our next bit of entertainment."

"Let him go, Ian," she growled.

"Only if you cooperate and play my game, Beloved."

There was a time he could bring her quivering to her knees with that word. She should have guessed from the beginning he was behind everything, but she'd worked so hard to forget those dark times. So hard that reality didn't register in her brain until it was too late.

"What game?" she snapped. Rage surfaced again when she spotted her toys scattered all over her couch. The bastard had been through her private belongings.

Again.

"I want you as naked as your sub." Ian leered. "Start taking off your clothes, or I start burning more than your plaything's hair." The blue flame inched closer to Rick's face.

However, he didn't move. "You know what he did to the cat, Johanna. He's not going to let us go." Rick's way of telling her to run. Now.

She gave a subtle shake of her head. He was in danger and hurt because of her. She wasn't going to leave him.

"You killed Patches?" Miranda pointed at Johanna. "Just to scare her?"

"They're lying, baby," Ian crooned. "You know I wouldn't hurt you."

An idea came to Johanna. The elastic in her bra wouldn't give her as much control as her personal whips on the couch. But it would still be painful.

"Fine." Johanna held up her hands. "Just please don't hurt him."

Apparently, she put enough whine into her voice Ian bought it. "Take off your clothes."

She unbuttoned her cuffs and started on the ones in front.

"Hurry up!" Miranda yelled.

"She's doing just fine, baby." Ian's lecherous expression pissed off Johanna even more. "She remembers how I like it after all this time."

"It's not my fault you were stupid enough to hit me in front of witnesses." Johanna countered her words by letting her blouse slowly slide down her arms.

Ian didn't answer. He licked his lips in anticipation.

"You've already had her," Miranda mewled as Johanna unhooked her bra. "I get to fuck her first."

Johanna pulled off her bra before she gave Miranda a side-eye once over. "I don't do girls, and you're not worth changing my mind."

Miranda shrieked at the insult.

Johanna snapped her bra at Miranda's face. One of the bra's hooks caught the younger woman in the eye. She let out a shrill scream. Johanna grabbed the bitch by the hair and slammed Miranda's head into her own rising knee. There was a loud crack of bone, and Miranda dropped to the floor like a sack of potatoes.

Rick rocked up on the balls of his feet, scooted a couple of centimeters, and slammed one of the chair legs onto Ian's instep. Johanna winced at the multiple crunching sounds.

But she was already racing for her black and red single tail.

Ian shoved Rick. The chair teetered, and both Rick and the chair crashed to the floor. Ian reached for the blowtorch which had fallen out of his grip and was currently searing her lovely blue Persian rug.

With a flick of her wrist and a twist of her hips, the tip bit into Ian's hand. He howled in pain. A total wuss. Not even a true dom. What the hell had she ever seen in him?

Johanna crossed to the blowtorch, turned it off, and set it on the counter before she stamped out the embers of her beautiful rug. Ian reached for what looked like a metal cricket bat, but a few snaps of her whip convinced him that was a poor decision. She grabbed the bat and tossed it onto the couch.

"Are you all right?" she asked as she untied Rick.

He grinned up at her. "As much as I like the idea of two of you, I think I need an ambulance."

Chapter Thirty-seven

The following Tuesday, Rick and Johanna joined Jamie and the emir for lunch. Rick gazed at Johanna as she filled the emir in on the events since he talked her into accepting Rick's expertise. Not that she needed that much help. Just thinking about her topless and driving Addington back with her whip turned him on.

It was a little hard to believe how much his entire life had changed in the last week.

The emir chuckled when she finished the tale, including the arrests of Addington and Miranda Hucklebee. According to Inspector Dunham, the two couldn't tattle enough on each other. Still, the worst of their crimes was the murder of Alice Hucklebee.

"I am glad to learn you did not inflict the damage on Mister Paine's face," the emir said.

"Faddil! You know I'm not that cruel," she replied.

"I am simply glad you are both alive," Faddil said. "And I wanted to see you one more time."

Johanna's alarmed expression matched Rick's worry. "Is something wrong?"

"I am headed home." He gave a heavy sigh. "The peace talks last week failed. I fear war is coming, and I may not be back to England for a while. And on that note, I must catch my plane."

The emir rose. The rest of the table followed suit.

He kissed Johanna on both cheeks before he shook Rick and Jamie's hands. "May Allah watch over all you until we meet again." He paused. "May I speak with you privately, Mister Paine?"

Confused, Rick shot a look at Johanna. She gave a subtle lift of her right shoulder. So, she didn't know what was going on either.

Rick followed the emir into the foyer of the restaurant. The Kutom head of security Hosni stood nearby. "Is there something else I can help you with, Your Majesty?" He wanted to return the bonus the emir paid him on top of his usual fees, but Jamie warned him that would insult the emir and cause an international incident.

"Consider this a wedding present since I may not be able to attend the actual ceremony." The emir withdrew an envelope from his jacket pocket.

"I think you are jumping ahead a little, Your Majesty." Rick stared at the white envelope and then at the emir. "We haven't even been on a proper date."

"Then you are truly a fool if you don't intend to serve her until the last of your days," the emir said. "Or you could take this and woo her properly. Either way this is a gift." He grabbed Rick's shoulder and kissed both cheeks. The left kiss hurt like hell with the three day old bruises and the recent dental work, but he managed not to wince.

The emir strode out of the foyer.

"That means he likes you and expects you to take care of Doctor Ridgeley." Hosni winked at Rick before he followed the emir.

Rick sucked in a deep breath before he slid a finger under the flap and pulled out the slip of paper inside. The cheque had an obscene number of zeros after the initial number. He replaced the cheque, folded the envelope and slid it into his inside jacket pocket.

He headed back into the restaurant's main dining area. He hoped Jamie had the name of a good investment banker.

A year later . . .

The sun warmed the back of Rick's neck and his shoulders as he guided his convertible north on the highway. The sweet smell of wildflowers had replaced the smell of petrol over an hour ago. He'd stopped to ditch the cans tied to his bumper before they left London proper. The noise would've driven him mad if he left them on all the way to Glasgow. He glanced at his bride, and he couldn't help smiling.

"Why are you grinning like a fool?" Johanna asked.

"How can I not be?" He laughed. "I still can't believe you said yes."

"To which question? Yours or the club's?"

"Actually, both of them," he admitted.

She held up her hand and examined her wedding band. Three diamonds set in a triskelion pattern of a platinum ring. Rick's matching band was three obsidian gems set in gold. It had taken a bit of convincing, but in the end, Johanna agreed most people wouldn't understand the symbolism of their wedding rings.

"You do know they are grooming you for a director's position," she said.

"Does that bother you?" he asked.

"No, it doesn't." She started pulling pins from her wedding updo. "There needs to be diversity on the club's board. However, if you decide to accept, we will need to renegotiate our boundaries regarding club activities."

"Of course, Mistress." Rick drove another kilometer, enjoying the flutter of her locks as they brushed against his cheek in the wind, before he added, "You do realize they plan to convince you to accept a director's position as well, don't you?"

"Of course, they are." She chuckled

"Does that mean you'll accept?" He glanced at her again. A sly look crossed her face.

"I already tell you what to do," Johanna said. "Or are you afraid some-one will take your place if you get a promotion at the club?"

"I would prefer you didn't replace me," he replied.

"There's a little side road to the left two kilometers ahead leading to a seldom-used picnic area."

"You're hungry?"

"You could say that." She was already wiggling out of her panties de-spite the seatbelt still latched in place. "Our honeymoon is officially start-ing. Now, are you going to turn where I tell you or do I have to punish you when we get to Glasgow?"

"Can't we do both?"

Johanna laughed, and her joy was the only thing to beat a beautiful day in May.

Excerpt from

Voil Jeanette
©2020, Onné Andrews

Jean hopped off the street car at her stop and rushed to her apartment. She couldn't bear to look at the pages Démas had given her until she was secure in her own room. Excitement battled fear in her stomach. She was so close to her goal, but what was the price really going to be for the knowledge she desired?

She unlocked the front door and jogged up the staircase of the Old Victorian. It had been divided into four tiny apartments. The upstairs was hotter than hell in the summer, but Jean and Demaria could afford it on their TA stipends.

Jean rattled their brass doorknob. Either her roommate was still at the library or she'd finally learned to lock the apartment door. Jean flipped to the apartment-specific key, inserted it in the lock, and twisted. She shoved the door open. No music flooded the apartment.

"Demaria?" She closed the door and turned the deadbolt. "Demaria?"

Nothing. Thank god, she wasn't home yet.

Jean headed to her bedroom. On second thought, she closed and locked her bedroom door, too. This wasn't something she wanted to share with Demaria. At least not yet.

Maybe not ever. Not that she thought her roommate would judge her. But Jean wasn't exactly comfortable with this side of herself either.

She flung her bag on the bed and pulled off her jean jacket. Maybe looking at this contract wasn't such a good idea. She could simply not read it. Rip it up. Then she wouldn't be tempted.

Why was she so obsessed with the idea of a private club that catered to every dark desire she carried in her heart?

Because maybe, just maybe, she'd find a place where people wouldn't look at her like she was depraved. Where a lover might understand her. Where she'd find a place to fit in.

Jean flopped on her bed, retrieved the stapled sheets from her bag, and pulled her knees to her chest. The first three pages were a questionnaire. What she liked. What she didn't like. What she was willing to try.

The next several pages were a non-disclosure agreement. She couldn't reveal anything she saw at the club, neither actions nor people. Well, "the establishment" were the words in the contract. Nowhere were the words "Club Noir" mentioned. Maybe she wasn't the only one disturbed by their sexual desires.

The last few pages were her training schedule. Her heart pounded. Three hours a day starting tomorrow was one thing. But on Friday, she would have to live with Démas twenty-four hours a day until the Mardi Gras party.

Jean bit her lower lip. She couldn't do it. It would mean missing classes on Monday and Tuesday. She couldn't afford to lose the pay. Not and be able to pay her rent. She was already on a bean and rice diet to stretch her stipend. She flopped on her bed and stared at the ceiling. All of her work tracking down Club Noir had been for nothing.

Now, what would she do? Her dissertation needed to be turned in to her advisor by May 1st. Could she really throw away her hard work over a couple of days of pay? And what about paying back her student loans? If she didn't finish her doctorate, it would be damn near impossible to land any counseling position.

Not to mention, what would she say to Demaria about being gone for all of Mardi Gras? They were supposed to go to a party together on Fat Tuesday.

And yet . . .

The need to go through with Démas's conditions was overwhelming. She was getting wet just thinking about being at his mercy. All he needed was that deep, sexy voice. It didn't matter what he looked like. Maybe he would keep her blindfolded during training, and—

Jean tossed the stapled contract across the room. She thought that subject of her thesis would help her get over her feelings, but it just seemed to make everything worse.

She flopped back on her bed. Maybe she was looking at this the wrong way. Maybe she needed to go through the reality of being at Démas's mercy. Learn that her fantasies and real sadistic discipline were two very different things.

Jean pushed herself upright, stood, and retrieved the contract. She grabbed the bright red pen she used to grade the undergraduates' papers. With a deep breath, she started filling out Démas's forms. When she reached the signature page, she hesitated.

If she signed the contract, there was no turning back. She'd have to confront her desires head on. In some ways, that would be so much harder than confronting her fears.

It would mean admitting she was a pervert.

Tears rolled down her cheeks. It would mean other people would know exactly what she was. Could she handle the derision she was sure would come? The mocking? The embarrassment?

Of course, you know what Jean's decision will be, but is the experience everything she desires? Or her worst nightmare? Find out in *Voil Jeanette,* the first volume of Club Noir Mardi Gras, coming to a retailer near you in 2021!

ONNÉ ANDREWS is currently trapped in a tiny Great Lakes town and writes erotic fiction to keep from turning into Stephen King's Carrie. Her men, Pierce and Daniel, feed her cheesecake in bed to calm the monster within her.

www.ingramcontent.com/pod-product-compliance
Lightning Source LLC
Chambersburg PA
CBHW070545100726
47907CB00004B/1273